A SOFT TOUCH

A NOTE ON THE AUTHOR

Anne Dunlop was born in Castledawson, County Derry Northern Ireland in 1968. She graduated in Agricultural Science at University College Dublin in 1991 and then returned to Northern Ireland to do postgraduate work.

Anne Dunlop is the author of the bestselling novel, *The Pineapple Tart,* also published by Poolbeg.

A
SOFT TOUCH
ANNE DUNLOP

POOLBEG

All characters and events in this novel are entirely fictitious and bear no relation to any real person or actual happening. Any resemblance to real characters or to actual events is entirely accidental.

First published 1993 by
Poolbeg Press Ltd
Knocksedan House,
Swords, Co Dublin, Ireland
Reprinted 1993
10 9 8 7 6 5 4 3 2

© Anne Dunlop 1993

The moral right of the author has been asserted.

The publishers gratefully acknowledge the financial assistance of
the Arts Council of Northern Ireland

A catalogue record for this book is available from the British Library.

ISBN 1 85371 237 X

Cover design by Wendy Robinson
Set by Mac Book Limited in Stone 10/14
Printed by Cox & Wyman Ltd, Reading, Berks.

For Trevor

Acknowledgement

Aidan C Shore for patience, instruction, and the loan of his word processor.

CHAPTER ONE

Richard Knight visited me today.

Most unexpected. I could have organised at least a blue moon in the sky had I known he was coming.

I expected to feel something when I saw him. Something other than bewilderment and irritation. Irritated because I wasn't wearing any lipstick and my fry was just ready to eat.

A couple of years ago when we were at UCD together I fancied myself tremendously in love with Richard but it must have been my imagination because the earth didn't move once all day. After some trying conversation we took a drive and had tea in a teashop in Dungannon.

"Tea for two," said Richard and I waited for a foolish grin to explode over my face but it didn't. We did the *Irish Times* crossword over tea because my conversation was exhausted and Richard could never lower himself to small talk.

Fickle love. When she strikes with her poisoned arrows I thought the puncture mark remained forever. Mummy and daddy are still in love. Daddy still fondles her bum when he passes her and she still enjoys it. No modesty in my mother. She just grabs him for a snog when the notion takes her. They are having their second honeymoon at present, except this time mummy says there will be no accidents. They accidentally made a baby the last time.

"When you marry," mummy used to advise, "choose your honeymoon carefully. Somewhere where there is lots to do so you don't do lots of what we did."

Now, less optimistically, she says, "Should you marry, Helen..."

Poor mummy. She can't work out what she did wrong. Three spinsters still under her roof. Daddy says it's because she educated us and he accepts no responsibility for it. He'd rather we had left school at sixteen and gone to the factory to stitch shirts. I tried to get a summer job there once to please him but they wouldn't accept me. Something to do with my eyesight they said. It was a shaming experience. I think I am the only person they ever rejected. Daddy says if we had gone to the shirt factory (I could have folded the shirts while the others stitched them) we would have caught husbands by the time we were twenty.

Laura has a husband, of course, but she ran away from him and lives at Derryrose with us. To be a runaway wife is much more romantic than a spinster. It gives the impression that she is a misused woman, that Lee was bad to her, that he beat her and kept her barefoot and pregnant. In actual fact he was too soft. She might have stayed longer if he had given her the odd thumping. Laura loves a bit of excitement. She was last seen hacking her way across the farmyard in a gaping négligé and wellie boots to the milking-parlour for consultation with Daisy. Laura hates Richard; bloody Richard she calls him. She thinks Richard broke my heart.

Daisy and Sarah, my spinster sisters, think so too. When Sarah discovered Richard in the kitchen she swore.

"God," she said, though she is a pinnacle of respectability usually and has taught Sunday school for years: nine-year-olds who memorise and re-gurgitate catechism for her and call her Ms Gordon because she is a feminist. Terrible waste, Sarah being a feminist. She is a very pretty girl but frustrated. So frustrated she is diseased with cleaning mania. "Doing her martyr act," says Laura. Sarah too was last seen hoofing it across the yard to the milking-parlour.

Daisy is milking the cows. Since our parents went away she has metamorphosed from an airhead into a farmer. I am supposed to help her but when I offer she smiles her sweet vague smile and in the nicest possible way tells me to keep off her patch. She always liked Richard when we were at UCD. I imagine she is restraining Laura and Sarah in case they return in force to tar and feather him.

Too late. Richard stood up and left about twenty minutes ago. Typical Richard he didn't even say goodbye. Anything emotional petrifies him. Once, when I was in love with him I tried to seduce him but he spanked me. Laura always said that if I had danced naked in front of him he wouldn't have noticed. He can talk about the price of barley exhaustively but mention happiness or sadness, any human emotion, and his barriers go up and he struggles to escape. He had escaped. I don't want him any more.

I couldn't sleep that night, the night after Richard Knight visited. I lay in bed fretting, tossing, turning, thinking the sleepless thoughts of insomnia. I didn't think of Richard of course. I brainstormed my eating habits. Atrocious. An entire diet consisting of lemon tea and toast. I had drunk four pots of lemon tea and eaten two toasted cheese and beetroot sandwiches today. And a cherry bun in the teashop in Dungannon. Possibly I was deficient in all the popular vitamins; probably my digestive, circulatory and respiratory systems were on the verge of collapse. When was the last time I had eaten properly? When I was convalescing last autumn I suppose, after the brain haemorrhage, the "near miss."

Mummy had once worked as receptionist in the doctor's clinic and so appointed herself my nutritionist and nurse. Nondescript nursing, questionable cookery. I had existed on raw eggs and cans of draught Guinness. Really. I drank the eggs and she drank the Guinness. Then she would dash to the bathroom to brush her teeth so daddy couldn't smell drink off her breath.

Here I was, riddled with incurable diseases, and

not a vitamin tablet in the house. There was royal
jelly which mummy had bought on special offer but
it had constipated her, so none of the rest of us risked
it. There was evening-primrose oil for pre-menstrual
tension and Korean ginseng and seaweed kelp and
garlic capsules because mummy claimed alternative
medicine made her feel sexy. Probably if I snooped
around in her bedroom I would find health food
aphrodisiacs and a window box full of marijuana
plants. The last time I had snooped I was ten and
confined to mummy's bed with measles. Bored being
sick I discovered Santa Claus at the bottom of the
wardrobe, a shattered illusion of childhood.
Intelligently I told no one and Santa still kept leaving
presents though we were now all old enough to be
Santa Claus ourselves. My sisters and I fervently
believed in him.

Once Laura had been snooping, looking for stray
10p's under the bed and found a packet of condoms.

"Can you imagine them at it?" We were in
premature adolescence at that stage; it was a wonder
we recognised our discovery.

"Oh yes," I had informed her, feeling mature, even
then, about *it*. "Even old people fancy each other,
Laura."

Too warm now. Got out of bed. Opened a window.
Not even a tremor of the real problem escaped.
Engrossed with my deficiencies and planning to drive
to the town tomorrow and buy some healthy food.
Saturated with resolve, desperate to flee this sleepless

night, I went downstairs to make a cup of Horlicks. With mummy gone honeymooning it was possible to roam Derryrose after dark without interference. Mummy was the terror of the sleepless night. She always heard me, and demanded the details of my movements, and then bombarded me with the usual instructions about checking that the back door was locked and switching off the lights.

The milk boiled over while I composed my list so I drank a glass of gooseberry wine instead, and, half cut, rolled back into bed. My last thought was that, maybe I was a diabetic because I was always thirsty. I had had mumps as a child; they could have destroyed my pancreas.

What was it Pope had said? A little learning is a wicked thing? Or was it a dangerous thing? Aunt May, teetotaller, Bible-thumper and bore, said alcohol killed brain cells. She didn't need a degree to know that.

I slept with hot bright dreams chasing round my head and woke tired and bored with myself. Thin rain spat through the window I had opened as an insomniac. Sarah was singing "Like a Virgin" in the bathroom. She obviously hadn't been down to the kitchen to witness the mess I had left with the boiled milk.

I met her on the landing.

"Helen," a firm voice of assertiveness. Sarah had gone to Fermanagh on a leadership course once. She hadn't been the same since. She spoke with the tone I used house-training a pup. "Helen, go back to your room and take those jeans off. They are mine. The last time you wore them you put grass stains on the knees."

"I was weeding strawberries the last time. It's too wet to weed anything today."

It is fruitless to argue with Sarah.

"Now, Helen!"

Meekly I did as I was told. She was going to be really cross with me when she saw the cooker. God forbid, she might sulk for days.

But the cooker was shining when I slunk into the kitchen and Daisy had just wet tea.

"You didn't sleep last night," she said in a soft, sympathetic voice.

I cringed.

"No. I was too hot. Give me the teapot. I don't like stewed tea."

I was waiting for her to mention Richard.

"I think I'm vitamin deficient," I said, making conversation. Sarah, having neatly hung her jeans up, had joined us and was measuring sugar-free muesli into a bowl. "Please can I have your car, Sarah? Please. I would cycle but I would be washed away in this rain." Being obsequious to please her. I'm not too proud to crawl when I want something. Sarah was relatively generous with her car but only because she extracted petrol money from us with Nazi-like ruthlessness.

"Hmm," said Sarah cynically.

"I'll even hoover the stairs when I get back," I offered in desperation.

"You said you would hoover them yesterday."

Oh no, now she was going to mention Richard.

"And you didn't sleep last night," she added. "I heard you banging about. Were you drunk again?" She scrutinised my guilty face. "You can have the car as long as you put petrol in it."

Escaped and alone in Magherafelt I went swimming. Strange that the woman charged me as an Under-18, but of course I said nothing. Would have been cheeky, me being so young. Mummy had sold me her swimsuit before she went on her second honeymoon. Suspicious, I suppose, but she only wanted a fiver and a Gordon never looks a gift horse in the mouth. Only when I was in the water did it become clear why the swimsuit was so cheap. The damned thing was see-through when it was wet.

I hate the overweight middle-aged ladies who paddle widths. I hate banging into them and having to apologise as if it was my fault. I want to hold a plump mermaid under and drown her to scare the others off.

I hated the green-goggled hairy monster swimming lengths beside me. I hated him touching me when we swam past each other.

"What a good stroke you have." He chatted me up as we stopped for a breather at the same time. "You can stroke me any time," he added so I exited the pool and changed for Wellworths.

There was a horrible queue in Wellworths. Tired now and temperamental I set my shopping basket on the floor to examine a shelf of vitamin supplements. I was reading the back of a jar of Vitamin B6 when the old man in front of me tripped over my basket and fell on his mouth and nose on the tiles and squashed his pan loaf and carton of milk beneath him.

Sexual harassment and murder in one afternoon. An exciting life I lead.

The housewives in front of me gathered round the sprawled body in silence. Murder to make their messages more memorable. I might be on *Scene Around Six* or in the *Belfast Telegraph*.

I got down on the floor beside the motionless man and pretended to feel for his pulse. The manager arrived, a nasty little man—bit of an upstart, mummy said. He looked nasty.

"Are you his daughter?"

"Not quite." With the innocent face of an under-eighteen and the quick wits of an old hand I said, "He tripped over that basket of photograph frames. It's rather precariously positioned, isn't it?"

"That's right," said a woman I could not have failed to notice. She wore flaming orange lipstick. "I stubbed my toe on that basket too." She pointed to a flaming orange toenail peeping from the toe of her white sling-back stiletto. These orange accessories coordinated with her orange, lemon and purple shellsuit. Shellsuits of that colour scheme had been following me round all morning; the Club Book was doing a roaring trade.

In a chorus, like a pack of football hooligans, the hitherto silent housewives spoke for me: "Disgrace. Claim. Damages."

So none of them liked the nasty little manager.

Then the old man coughed. So he was alive. So he could defend himself.

"Thank you very much," I said to the orange-shellsuited woman as we packed our bags together. "That manager could have got nasty."

She grinned. "I enjoyed it love. He wouldn't change a toaster I bought in the sale a month ago, even though I had my receipt. I hope the old boy puts in a claim against him."

"Sure," she added, "I would have tripped over your shopping basket myself if I had thought of it before he did."

CHAPTER TWO

Derryrose was silent and steamed up when I got back from Magherafelt. Hearing me, however, Sarah shot into the kitchen, rubber-gloved, face of agitation.

"Don't panic," I said. "I put petrol in the car."

"Something terrible has happened."

Something terrible was always happening to Sarah.

"Have a cup of tea," I offered. "Has Laura finally got out of bed?"

Laura would have lain in bed until she rotted but nobody cared because when she was in bed she had her babies in bed with her and when they were in bed you could not hear Scarlett crying. The twins were almost six months old and Scarlett had cried continuously since the moment of her birth. A crying baby, like a nagging mother, wears you away.

"No thank you, Helen." Sarah never drank tea. She drank pint glasses of water to flush the toxins from her body. But the DOE were changing the water pipe along our road and the tap water tasted and smelled like vomit.

The news was bad.

"Mummy and daddy phoned to say they are

coming home."

"Why?"

"Why are they coming home? Daddy's chest is bad again. Very inconsiderate of him. I thought they would be gone for at least another month. They haven't had a honeymoon since they were married."

"I bet they have squandered all their money," I said. "You know what the price of drink is like in the Republic. And mummy goes mad for a well-pulled pint."

"Quite," said Sarah who disapproved of mummy's exploits with Guinness. "But I really think the problem is daddy's chest. He was wheezing on the telephone."

Daddy's chest had always been weak, living with him in the damp of Derryrose. Last winter was very wet and he had to draw himself up a rota in case he overdosed on the steroids that were being pumped into him. It was rather like the rota he made for getting up at night when the ewes were lambing, so complicated that he never understood it, and so it got filed away and forgotten after a week. He resorted to inhaling before going out anywhere. A type of ritual: hairspray on the hair, a suck at the inhaler. It looked as if he was using mouthwash. Laura thought he was so vain the day mummy permed his hair (because he felt it would sit better with a bit of a curl) that she offered to pluck his eyebrows for him.

Sarah was so upset she was eating a piece of wheaten left on the table since breakfast. "They lack organisation," she informed me. "Didn't give a time.

They might call in on Granny McBride on the way through Moneymore, they said. Or they might not come today at all."

"Well they must still be speaking to each other if they are willing to visit Granny McBride."

Granny McBride was mummy's mummy and she had been in the old people's home since we were little children.

"I wanted to go to Ballymena this afternoon," said Sarah sullenly. "I have to get books before school starts. How can I go now? The house is filthy. Mummy will think we were having orgies. I've just cleaned the bathroom. I had to scrape the scum off round the bath."

"If you are going to Ballymena I'll come too," I said cheerfully. Marvellous how a trip, even to Ballymena, can generate excitement. "I can search the charity shops for an alternative birthday present for Daisy."

"The stairs still need hoovering, Helen."

"If we go now," I said, "we'll have all afternoon to clean the house."

"Right," said Sarah briskly. She was always brisk after she decided on something. Throwback to the leadership course. "Right. I will just run upstairs and wake Laura. She is a disgrace. I don't believe she has changed out of her nighty since mummy and daddy went on honeymoon."

"She did. The day she signed on the dole."

"No, she did not. She pulled a tracksuit over it. I

know because she made me drive her into Magherafelt
and sit in the car with the twins. And I drove her into
Castledawson last night to buy chips. And I had to go
into the chip shop for her because she was wearing
purple shoes, pink socks and red tracksuit bottoms."

"No one would have noticed, Sarah."

"She wasn't wearing a bra, and you know what a
big girl she is," said poor Sarah who couldn't cope
with a wanton display of secondary sexual char-
acteristics.

Sarah refuses to frequent charity shops in case she
catches a disease. We parted at the Tower Centre and
she warned me she would go home without me if I
wasn't at Dunnes Stores by half past three. Sarah is
tough like that.

Oxfam had exactly what I was looking for,
matching picture frames for Daisy's flower pictures,
10p each. Daisy would be delighted with me. Indeed
I was delighted with myself.

Sarah was late. I had eaten two ice-creams at
Dunnes Stores by the time she arrived, hyper-
ventilating.

"Get out of my way, you snivelling brat," she yelled
at a toddler foolish enough to get in her way. When
the child's mother opened her mouth to protest Sarah,
in her most pedantic elocution voice, said, "Keep
that infant under control, madam, and kindly stop
chewing with your mouth hanging open."

"Sarah, Sarah," I led her away from the potentially
volatile situation. What had happened her? She was

out of control.

"Couldn't you find the books you wanted?"

"I got the books." In the claustrophobic familiarity of her brown Mini Metro she relaxed.

"I saw Ian Flemming."

Once upon a time Sarah had been engaged to Ian Flemming, a very suitable, sadly impotent accountant. Fortunately for all concerned she had discovered this in time.

But the experience had scarred her. She became a feminist and renounced menfolk.

"Helen, I could be Mrs Flemming. That fat, moist, lardy man could be my husband."

"You had a lucky escape," I contributed. "I hope you ran away when you saw him coming?"

A favourite trick of mine, to run away from anything I couldn't confront. As a child I used to hide in the outside loo after dinner to avoid being told to wash the dishes.

Ian had descended on her and extended a soft wet hand. Christian friendship, he called it.

"Ian?" I said. "Good-living?"

"We only slept together after we were engaged. Only a few times. Furtively like it was something bad. We didn't discuss the details."

"He never looked like he would be any good at it," I comforted. "Laura wanted to buy him *The Joy of Sex* when you got engaged."

"It would have done him no harm," she said spitefully.

Ian had insisted on buying coffee. And on telling her of the mission he was organising in a tent in Castledawson. He wanted Daisy to play the piano at the mission.

"Will he pay her well?"

"Don't be so innocent, Helen," she reprimanded me. "Daisy will get her reward in heaven. Take off your rose-coloured spectacles."

Daisy threw a major wobbly when Sarah mentioned the mission. Daisy used to be so sweet and so easily manipulated. Now we were all so cynical.

"Where is Laura?" I asked. It was after four o'clock. Not even Laura lay in bed that long.

"Laura appeared at lunchtime," said Daisy. "She claims to be poisoned by Tommy Miller's chips."

"And the twins?"

"She says they have slept all day. It would be madness to disturb Scarlett."

Laura, green yet comfortable, was lying in bed reading a trashy novel. The curtains were drawn against the rain and the lights and fire lit. She reminded me of the seductress in Thomas Hardy's *The Woodlanders*, but I couldn't remember the name. Shaun was lying naked on the lino floor. Laura saved on nappies by cleaning up after him as if he was a dog.

Scarlett the Screamer was still asleep.

"I am poisoned," Laura announced. "Never let me near Tommy Miller's chip shop again, not if I threaten you with the bread knife. I am so ill I couldn't eat the liver in the fridge. Reminded me of Dublin, the liver."

"Sarah met Ian Flemming in Ballymena," I told her to change the subject. I didn't want Laura's reminiscences to degenerate to Dublin and to bloody Richard and to why he had been allowed over the threshold of Derryrose yesterday.

"No," Laura was delighted. "How is the World's Greatest Lover?"

I told her.

"Poor Daisy," she laughed. "Imagine her in a knitted beret thumping out 'Abide With Me' and Ian preaching on fornication and sins of the flesh." She winked at me. "We'll have to go."

"Daisy is refusing," I said firmly. "She says they make you pray in public."

"I know, I know," said Laura suddenly. "I know who Daisy can delegate."

"Who?"

"The Rabbit. I caught her at the dole office the last day I signed. She was so embarrassed to see me. You know what a social-climbing snob she is. She used to play the piano at Sunday school. She would be honoured to be asked."

The Rabbit, Sandra Jackson, had been in Laura's class at school. She was Laura's friend. Laura was not her friend. We knew her socially. She was a nice girl. We all hated her, except Sarah who was a hypocrite and pitied her.

Laura smiled at my inspiration. "Brilliant. Bloody

brilliant. She has invited herself to tea tomorrow. We'll volunteer her then."

"Mummy and daddy will be home tomorrow."

"No," said Laura poking her head through the curtains like a peeping Tom, "mummy and daddy are home now, they have just driven up."

"Damn," I said. "And I still haven't hoovered the stairs."

CHAPTER THREE

Mummy was wearing black shades and pink lipstick. She had met a woman in Wellworths—mummy knew that the cupboard was always bare at Derryrose—and the woman had told her that she had seen her and daddy's photograph in the "Memory Lane" section of the *Mid-Ulster Observer*. Excited like children, mummy and daddy had forgotten the shopping and had hared out of Wellworths to the nearest newsagents to buy the paper.

"We thought they would be suspicious at us buying a Catholic newspaper," said mummy, "so I wore my shades as a disguise."

The photograph had been taken at a dance before they married. Daddy hadn't changed a bit in nearly thirty years. Mummy if anything was better-looking now...

"You look better now," said Sarah critically. "Your face is thinner and you suit the crew cut better than a bouffant."

Mummy was delighted. She even called daddy "pet."

Their honeymoon had been a tremendous success.

They had stopped in Newry on the way home, and mummy had bought daddy three pairs of shoes costing £4 each in the sale.

"We do have a reason for coming home," said daddy. "We are going to build a house."

"But you have a house," Daisy, Sarah and I chorused. "This house."

"This house is cold and damp and it's ruining your father's chest. We thought of a brown-and-white bungalow at the bottom of the drive."

"So you can still keep an eye on us?" Laura fully dressed and with a baby under each armpit had come into the kitchen.

"Exactly; and I haven't too far to walk to hunt your boyfriends if they stay later than twelve on Saturday night." Mummy smiled bravely as Laura deposited the Screamer on her lap. Scarlett looked like a pixie in her red romper suit and straggling fair hair but the wicked glint in her eye made her seem more like a goblin.

"When we went up to Donegal to visit your father's Aunt Maisie the roads were littered with clean little brown-and-white bungalows."

All her life mummy had aspired to be awarded the title "Nice Modest Wee Woman." It hadn't happened and it wasn't likely to. Perhaps she thought that if she lived in a clean little bungalow she would be considered a clean little woman, which was nearly as prestigious as being a nice modest wee one.

"The bungalow is going to have central heating,

hot water and insulation in the roof," said daddy, "And double-glazing and a damp course."

"You'll suffocate," said Daisy. "Seriously, you are used to the fresh air blowing through Derryrose— you'll never survive a hot house."

"We'll acclimatise."

"Will you have a spare room?" Sarah, hopefully. The idea of a clean, hot little house at the bottom of the drive was more than Sarah could bear.

"No," said daddy, "It's going to be our love-nest."

"But you can come for holidays," said mummy who always felt sorry for Sarah.

Daddy was in such a good mood he even made a joke. He was nursing his grandson at the time.

"Look," he said tipping Shaun. "This boy has six toes."

Daddy couldn't bring himself to call his grandson by his Fenian name. He said it choked in his throat.

We all investigated Shaun's feet. They were perfectly normal.

"Ha ha," laughed daddy, slapping his thigh and wheezing. "He has six toes but I didn't say they were on the same foot."

Oh God. My eyes met Laura's across daddy's head. He had finally flipped his lid. And mummy was no better. She was encouraging him. She was laughing.

"Speaking of completely mad," I interjected, "How is Aunt Maisie?"

"Worse," said mummy, immediately serious. "She didn't recognise the car when we pulled up. She was hanging out of an upstairs window yelling at us to 'Piss Off.'"

"You have left out the good bit," said daddy.

"Yes," said mummy, "It was gruesome. She was hanging out of the window naked. She must have been in bed because she was dressed when she came downstairs to let us in. She has six locks on the front door, you know, but all the downstairs windows were wide open."

"Maybe she was drunk," Sarah sniffed her disapproval. Great-aunt Maisie was certainly fond of her gin. "Life's small sweetener," she called it. I had had a hangover for a week the last time I visited.

"She needs company," said mummy looking at me significantly. "She likes you, Helen. She asked for you. Keep in there and she will leave you her fortune."

That night mummy and daddy decided to go dancing. Mummy put on a clean pair of white socks and her brown leather shoes with the half-inch heel. Daddy had however lost a bit of weight on his honeymoon (no explanation forthcoming); so he put on his pale grey suit, the one he wears when he is thinner. Usually the suit only fits after a month of lambing so he was delighted with himself. And he was wearing Uncle James's dancing shoes, swanky black slip-ons with a gold bar across the front. He sent mummy to remove the white socks and her corduroy trousers, and to tart herself up in a straight skirt, black high-heeled shoes and black stockings—the type of thing her friend

Ruth Paisley, the Trollop of the Town, wore shopping. Except the last time we saw Ruth in Magherafelt she had cigarette smoke flying from her nostrils and was wearing a black leather jacket and ankle chain to complete the ensemble. And Ruth drove a black 2.8 fuel injection Ford Capri and mummy drove a Morris. Mummy deviated from the Trollop effect somewhat by wearing a frilly blouse on top and a mohair hand-knitted cardigan. She looked almost like a Presbyterian but the look in her eye gave her away. A quick spray of hair lacquer and they were off. Three spinster daughters and a runaway wife waved from the front door.

Now I don't know what time the Jacksons have tea on Sunday but the Rabbit drove her clean little Fiesta through the gates of Derryrose about four the next afternoon. A saucy breeze had blown away the cloudy morning revealing blazing sunlight, and mummy and daddy had stripped to matching thermal vests to stroll around the lawn. Considering that daddy had yawned during church and mummy had picked at her nail varnish they had woken up considerably since lunchtime. I don't think they even noticed the Rabbit arrive.

Sarah and I had been reclining in the suntrap beside the front door, and Sarah, spying the Fiesta, ordered me indoors to cover myself. I was wearing more clothes than mummy but Sarah was insistent; because it was Sunday, she said. "I'm sure God doesn't notice how much clothing covers me," I grumbled getting up and setting down the *News of the World*.

"Possibly not but Sandra will notice and she gossips more than God. And Helen, for goodness sake, hide that trashy paper."

Laura who had been napping all afternoon stuck her head round the front door. "Not already, the nosy tart." She dumped Scarlett in Sarah's arms and instructed, "Stick something in her; make her scream."

"Where are you going?" I shouted after the retreating négligé in the hall.

"I'm going to have a stiff drink before I face her," shouted Laura. "Otherwise I will strangle that skinny throat. If you have any sense you will have one too."

When I returned to the front of the house, respectably clad in a horrid denim skirt that Sandra later admired, Sarah and Sandra were playing with the precociously well-behaved Scarlett and discussing the forthcoming mission in Castledawson.

"You remember Ian Flemming from school," I heard Sarah say. "He's doing the preaching you know."

"He has become such an enthusiastic young man," I added, "and so charismatic."

"And so sincere," added Sarah.

"Oh yes, I remember him," said the Rabbit. She had done something with her hair, streaked it perhaps. It was frizzy at the ends.

"You and he had a relationship, didn't you, Sarah?"

"We were very young." Sarah lowered her eyelashes

modestly.

"I believe he is looking for a pianist," I said casually. "He phoned here last night asking us to suggest someone. He said he wanted a steady, reliable, sincere person. Do you know anyone like that, Sandra?"

Laura was still in the sitting-room swilling beetroot wine when I went indoors to make tea.

"I can't face her today," she sighed. "And that temperamental tart Scarlett won't even cry when I ask her. She had me up the most of last night."

There was literally not a bite in the house to offer Sandra. Daisy was in the kitchen finishing the last of the soda bread before she went outdoors to do the milking.

"Go to the shop along the Toome line," she suggested. "It's run by Catholics so it will be open on a Sunday. I think they sell home-made cakes and things."

She grinned suddenly. "You had better take the Morris down the back lane and over the flat meadow to the road so she doesn't see you leaving. I bet she doesn't eat food bought on the sabbath."

Daddy's Morris was built when cars were made to last. He always drove her to the meadows to get the cows when he was milking and to check the ewes and lambs in summer. I can remember her bogging only once and that was because we were all in her at the time. We had been rounding up the ewes for shearing, and Daisy, sitting on the bonnet, had navigated him into a bit of wet bog. He sat in the driver's seat, revved a lot and hurled oaths at us for incompetence and inefficiency. Mummy had of course sulked, thrown down her bit of acetylene pipe and marched home. Once the car was finally out of the wet patch daddy had spent the rest of the day licking round her to be forgiven.

I appeared at the front door carrying a tray loaded with egg sandwiches, fruit-cake and tea. I overheard Laura's voice: "No I haven't been to Reverend Robinson for a while, Sandra. I have converted to the Church of Ireland," followed by the Rabbit's shocked squeak, "Have you considered this carefully, Laura? You know they are marching on the Road to Rome," followed by Laura's manic, "But the sermons are shorter."

Of course Laura hadn't converted. She was much too lazy to rise for the 10 a.m. service at the C of I and no way would she bob up and down and kneel on a board.

"There was wine and strawberries at the rectory at the start of July," she said as I poured the tea. "And Sandra, don't quote me, but I declare the reverend was tight."

"Laura," I chastised her, "You shouldn't spread such rumours—"

"—or tell such lies," I added *sotto voce*, handing her her tea.

"What a delicious cake," said Sandra daintily nibbling at an egg sandwich I had made from the loaf I bought along the Toome line. There had been only one bantam egg in the hen-house and I had had to stretch it with scallions and the top of the milk.

"Yes," I smiled. "It looks well doesn't it? It's a new recipe for fruit-cake that I haven't tried before."

"Lies," mouthed Laura at me, "and on a Sunday!"

The rotten cake disintegrated to crumbs when I cut it. Laura sniggered. "You must have left it in the oven too long, Helen."

Sarah was disgusted with us. Her body language was threatening and furtive ankle-kicking warned us that there would be slaps and tears when Sandra left if we didn't stop teasing her.

Sandra wanted us to go to the Port with her that night. She and her brother Johnboy Jackson always went to the prom on a Sunday night.

"You meet such nice people," she enthused. "It would do you the world of good to get out for an evening without the twins, Laura."

She sipped her tea, little finger raised delicately.

We declined.

"We are going to visit Granny McBride this evening," said Sarah, blushing because she doesn't tell lies as easily as Laura or me. Because any chat about mummy's mother is a taboo subject with nice people, Sandra said no more. It was handy sometimes having a skeleton in the family cupboard but we used it only in desperate circumstances.

"Poor Granny McBride," said Sarah after the Rabbit had left. "I hate to use her to get out of tight corners, but I couldn't bear to go to Portstewart tonight. Ian told me yesterday he was going to hold an open-air meeting there."

"Just as well your head isn't as soft as your heart then," said Laura. "Can you imagine being in the car with Sandra? I bet she plays Jim Reeves on the stereo. And that brother of hers is a half-wit."

"No he isn't." Sarah was cross. "He was at the Rainey with us. Don't be so mean Laura. I feel sorry for Sandra. She has been at a loose end since she lost her job in Belfast."

"Pity she didn't lose that Belfastie whine as well."

CHAPTER FOUR

Birthdays are a milestone in anyone's life. Daisy was no exception. To help her celebrate—she was twenty-four on 6 September—we decided to check out the new night-club in Portstewart. As I was to visit Aunt Maisie the following day it was also a send-off for me. In the end I had suggested I go to Aunt Maisie myself. Daddy wasn't so keen on the idea. He was afraid that Aunt Louise would disparage my intentions and accuse me of keeping in to get left the fortune. Personally I suspected that the fortune legend was a myth. If she ever had money, Aunt Maisie had drunk it long ago.

"It dates us somewhat," Daisy sighed, "that we are not too young any more to appreciate an older crowd."

We were in the bathroom at the time and she was washing her hair in Fairy Liquid because we had run out of shampoo. I was painting my toenails and waiting for her to finish so I could wash the conditioner out of my own hair.

"But not too old to appreciate a birthday cake."

Mummy, thinking she was old enough, had tried to wean Laura off the birthday cake idea when she was sixteen. Laura had cried her eyes out, and because it was an important issue we had all backed Laura and cried too. Enough said. A birthday cake was produced with every birthday since.

But there had been a hiccup during the preparations when the range temperature shot up and burnt Daisy's cake to a crisp. Resourcefully we had hacked the burnt bits off but what was left was still so charred even daddy couldn't eat it. At 5.25 p.m. Sarah was sent to Magherafelt to ransack the town and return with a cake. She brought back an out-of-date pineapple tart but that wasn't the point. It was the principle that mattered. We so rarely got real food at Derryrose that an out-of-date tart was better than no cake.

"Hurry up, Daisy. This conditioner has been on longer than one minute."

Daisy was having problems washing the Fairy Liquid out of her hair, "Yes, yes," she snapped. "But really, what sort of house is this? Seven bottles of conditioner in the bathroom cabinet and no bottles of shampoo."

When mummy heard that Caesar's had an older crowd she decided to come with us. She and Ruth (the Trollop) Paisley were coming, she said.

"No," we said, "You can't."

"But the lights will be dimmed," she protested. "No one will be able to see Ruth's wrinkles."

When she told daddy she was going he said, "Well, I hope you aren't planning to wear those white trousers. I can see your knicker-line through them."

"Who is going to baby-sit?" we asked, appealing to her maternal instincts. "It has been so long since poor Laura got out of the house. And daddy is dangerous with children."

When mummy was in hospital having me she left Laura for daddy to look after. He didn't change her nappy for two days.

It had been a close shave. She said she and Ruth were coming with us the next time.

Caesar's is one of those places where the casual man wears a shirt and tie and girls shiver in skirts that barely cover them. So for contrariness I wore a skirt to my ankles and a shirt that plunged to my navel.

My sisters and I propped up a mushroom and eyed the endless shirts and ties. There weren't any other girls as obviously interested as us. Most of them sat in tight little corners attracting attention by hysterical laughter.

"God love them," said Daisy who had been observing a particular party with scientific interest, "I may smell of cows and there may be Fairy Liquid in my hair but I hope I never have to resort to nervous laughter to catch a man."

The nervous laughter trick appeared to be working. The casual man wants a bubbly girl these days.

"Well," said Laura with admiration. "So that is what we have been doing wrong all along. To catch a man wearing a shirt and tie, you don't look available, you sound desperate."

"Let's go and dance round our handbags," I suggested. "We are out of our league here."

The music was good. I had no inhibitions dancing because I didn't care what the casual man or the hysterical girl or anyone thought of me. But it worked. I got noticed, and at the start of the next slow set a huge man asked me to dance. Starved so long for a bit of sex I didn't even bother to look at his face. I accepted immediately. As I moved off with him to the dance floor I overheard someone else, his friend perhaps, ask Sarah to dance. Men in these places always operate in couples not packs. More mature I suppose.

Sarah said, "I'll only dance with you if you promise not to grope me."

I made a mental note to teach her how to talk to boys.

Huge had acres of chest and I felt small in his arms. I banged my nose on his breast bone when another couple banged into us. They were eating each other, and didn't notice.

Huge smelled delicious—expensive aftershave I guessed. We talked and did not suck face. I have no idea what our conversation was about. I was on automatic, had been a tart for so long it came back naturally. Like riding a bicycle, you never forget. Familiar territory, flirting with an attentive man. Subconscious relaxation.

"Helen, what would you do with a man like that?" Daisy asked in awe after the slow set when Huge had gone to buy me a drink.

"Work or walk," scoffed Sarah. Sarah had had a nasty experience with her man. He had disregarded her "no-groping" threat and when he fondled her bum she had poked him in the eye.

"Oh Helen," giggled Laura, captivated, "he's so butch he's bound to be gay."

Laura always acted silly after a few drinks because she didn't get out that often.

"Huh," scowled Sarah, "He thinks with one organ only and it's not his brain."

I did not recognise Huge's face when he returned with my Diet Coke and blackcurrant (because I was driving home). But I did remember that he was distinctively ornamented with a navy sportscoat over his shirt and tie. I chatted away to him, delightful, charming, unobtainable. I didn't want to appear too available in case he suggested we retire to the back seat of his car for a bit of grunting and heaving.

I do not know where disc jockeys come from or if they must take exams to qualify. In a previous life I suspect that Caesar's DJ was the entertainments officer at a holiday camp.

"Hi, everybody," he crooned into the microphone. "It's fan-dabby-dozy to see you all here, enjoying Caesar's, the hottest nightspot on the Atlantic coast" (pause for applause). "Our talent scouts have been mingling with the crowd and at midnight they will be announcing the finalists in tonight's heat of 'Cleopatra of Caesar's.' Take it away, boys."

"'Cleopatra of Caesar's,'" repeated Daisy, contemplating. "I thought Cleopatra had a fling with Mark Antony? Do you think the talent scouts will choose Sarah as a finalist? She is easily the best-looking here."

"Not if the talent scout was the guy who tried to grope her," I answered looking over at Sarah who was artistically draped over a banister talking to a strange man. Possibly he was a talent scout, probably she was telling him to push off. It would be against Sarah's feminist principles to participate in anything as demeaning as a beauty competition. Which was a pity. Because the winner of that night's heat would win a dinner for two in Caesar's new restaurant.

"Why don't they have a wet T-shirt competition?" pouted Laura. "Then I could win a dinner in Caesar's restaurant. Your stale birthday cake has given me indigestion, Daisy."

Sarah, slightly flushed, stopped talking to the man and came over to where the rest of us were standing, Huge included, but Huge was temporarily forgotten. She was just so pretty, I thought, a natural beauty, that cost her a fortune to maintain.

She had to buy expensive glossy magazines to study the beautiful women and pricey clothes littering their pages. She had to travel to Ballymena every month to get her hair streaked and styled. No barber's shop in Magherafelt with the rest of us for a £2 trim. She had to frequent the classically expensive clothes shops in Belfast and buy the classically expensive make-up they kept protected behind glass windows in Magherafelt chemist shops. The plainer the packaging the dearer the product. And she wore a perfume that claimed to contain the "Essence of Woman." I had sprayed it over myself once when she was at school and it had brought my neck out in pimples.

"Was he a talent scout? Did you tell him to push off?" Daisy demanded.

"Yes; I mean yes, he was a talent scout but he was quite polite and very persistent so I agreed to be a finalist."

Laura was already *en route* to the bar to buy her a Martini so she would go through with it and give us a laugh.

"Oh Sarah," I teased, "You could be Cleopatra of Caesar's."

"Cleopatra had black hair, Helen, and she fancied Mark Antony, not Caesar."

At midnight, after three Martinis for courage, Sarah and five other finalists mounted the platform with the DJ. We had advised her to continue smiling no matter what he said. Sarah took queer notions sometimes and if she fancied a slight to either herself or her feminism she might conveniently forget she was a lady and cause a scene.

"She is easily the best-looking," we comforted each other and informed Huge.

Huge said he thought her unapproachably pretty.

"You're right," I agreed a bit anxiously. "Do you think she should titter behind her hand like the others?"

"Only if she wants to win," he said smiling at me.

Sarah came second. The winner was the noisiest bird at the hen-party that had been going on in the corner of the night-club. She was shorter than Sarah and had lipstick smeared on her teeth. We were disgusted but Sarah didn't seem to mind.

"There is a bottle of wine for the runner-up," she told us when she had descended from the platform and glory to join us. "I have to find Mr Caesar after the disco ends and he will give it to me."

"Did you enjoy yourself?" She looked less wooden than she had in a long time.

"Well, yes," she confessed, smiling her white-toothed even smile. There was no lipstick smeared on my sister's teeth.

"But I couldn't have done it without the Martini."

Even with all this excitement going on Huge must still have been charmed with me because he asked for my phone number. He had behaved so well all night I was afraid that he wasn't even going to kiss me at the end of the evening. So I kissed him. It was pretty good, eight out of ten, experienced and slick. I doubt he had clashed teeth with anyone in ten years. And walking him to the door of Caesar's filled in time while Sarah searched for Mr Caesar and her prize bottle of wine.

By the time she reappeared we were cold and fed up and Daisy and Laura were already complaining of hunger and had bullied me into agreeing to drive them to Kentucky Fried Chicken in Portrush before we went home.

"Where were you?" we demanded, mildly irritated.

"Oh, he wanted me to choose whatever bottle I wanted and when I told him I wanted a bottle of English wine he had to search the cellar to find it. He was most obliging."

"Are you sure he didn't pull the label off a bottle of cider and give you that?" Laura eyed the English wine suspiciously. "I have never heard of English wine, except for Concorde and even *I* won't drink it."

Outside the disco a mist of cobweb lace hung spectral on the car-park. Kissing Huge had done me the world of good. Revitalised my literary awareness. I was admiring the haunting glimmer of lights through the lace when Sarah said,

"Oh God, Helen, the car lights! You must have left them on."

Suddenly the mist was clawing damply at the cleavage of my shirt. And when the Morris sighed and groaned and grinded and sighed some more the dampness spread to beads of perspiration down my back.

"There is no point in pushing her," I told my sisters grimly, because I was waiting for them to jump me and tear me to pieces. "There isn't even a light when I switch on the ignition. We need jump leads. Sorry."

Sarah took command. "We have jump leads in the boot," she announced. "I threw them in before we left. I wouldn't travel anywhere in this car without taking precautions."

There were only a few cars still parked at Caesar's.

"I bet those cars are full of courting couples," giggled Laura. "Who is going to disturb their passion?"

"Helen"—they all nominated me together—"since you got us into this mess."

There was nothing else for it. I approached the nearest car, the other three trailing at a safe distance. Certainly there were signs of life. The windows were steamed up. Timidly I knocked the windscreen.

"Excuse me," I said, "Excuse me."

It was the DJ and the girl who had won the beauty competition, the one with lipstick on her teeth.

"Well, love," said the DJ, "what's your problem?"

I explained and miraculously, instead of telling me to go forth and multiply, he said, "That's your Morris, is it? You don't get cars like that any more. I learned to drive in one, same colour and all," and he forgot his bit of fluff in his eagerness to oblige.

The Morris started smartly and I drove to Portrush where Daisy, with characteristic benevolence, bought us all chickenburgers and chips with the £20 mummy and daddy had given her for her birthday. And Sarah, usually tight with money but with her latent generosity alerted by her glory, bought us cans of Coke though she warned they would make us burp and rot our teeth.

"So, Helen," asked Laura, "Are you going to see that man again?"

"Maybe," I answered through a mouthful of chicken, "Maybe."

CHAPTER FIVE

I had completely forgotten about Huge the next morning. We hadn't got back to Derryrose until after three and mummy had stormed my room and woken me before eight because she and daddy had decided to drive me to Donegal in the Morris rather than pay Sarah to take me in her Metro. I suspect that she wanted another opportunity to gloat over the brown-and-white bungalows and dream about her own, still embryo in her imagination. Mummy always gets hyper before a trip to Donegal because she thinks that Aunt Maisie patronises her. That morning she was wearing purple eye-shadow, navy mascara and sky-blue eyeliner. She has very short eyelashes because she claims to have shaved them off, aged thirteen, with a man's shaver trying to tidy her eyebrows. She says they never grew back. The colour scheme was more artistic than clashing to my mind anyway but Sarah shared her disapproval with me when we met in the bathroom later.

"She looks like a rainbow," Sarah said crossly because she had slept badly and had dreamed she won the beauty competition in Caesar's the night before and the prize had been a night in the DJ's car with him. We were both looking in the mirror at the same time and I noticed that there was absolutely no likeness between us.

Mummy and daddy and I all made an effort to behave on the way to Donegal. I was not allowed to drive. Daddy gave me a dissertation on "The Bantam Hen to Clock" and we stopped for picnics twice. The first picnic was eight miles from home; the second eight miles from Aunt Maisie's house because mummy and daddy were afraid that she wouldn't feed them, and they said her tea tasted like the flushing from a chemical toilet. The last time they had visited mummy had snooped a bit in the kitchen and found a pint of milk two months old, and a loaf of bread with blue mould growing on it. I thought mummy's brown-and-white bungalows were horrid little hen-houses.

Aunt Maisie was delighted to see me. She had been resting in the garden beneath a ridiculous straw hat when we drove up and she fussed and said that I looked tired and had got thinner.

"I'm so glad you haven't a mahogany tan dear," she patted my freckled hand maternally and scrutinised my mother's brown skin with obvious dismay. "Jennifer, you should try to avoid the sun at your age. You are in danger of resembling a wrinkled prune. Everywhere I go I see wrinkled women in every shade from orange to black."

"Oh, they are out of bottles," said mummy piqued. She was quite proud of her tan and wasn't used to having it criticised. "Mine is the real thing. And Helen looks pale and lethargic only because she was out half the night dancing."

Aunt Maisie behaved normally all afternoon. Mummy and daddy were mistaken. She was not off her rocker. She was cheeky with mummy and rude to daddy but that was perfectly normal. And she didn't offer to feed them but that was no more than they expected. She lay in the shade of a silver tree in the garden and smoked her cigarettes and watched the silver leaves blow across the lawn like white ashes. When my parents left she made a pot of Earl Grey tea and we drank it beneath the silver tree and watched the evening shadows lengthen towards us.

"How was the dance last night?" she asked eventually when the heat had gone out of the day and we were strolling through her magnificent dahlias to the house.

"I love orange dahlias," she added inconsequentially. "I love the way they glare. Such delightful vulgarity in this age of neutral modesty."

She smiled at me. "Did you meet a nice young man, dear?"

"Not so young," I smiled back. "But he kissed nice."

We had a herbal omelette with yogurt for dinner.

"I never thought that I would eat yogurt," said Aunt Maisie. "It's such a yuppy's food I always think. But there is a very nice girl in the shop in Ballybofey and she assures me that the Greeks have been eating it since the start of the world. That girl is wasted."

I told her about Sarah coming second in the beauty

competition the night before.

"And she eats a tub of natural yogurt every day," I added.

"Oh," sniffed Aunt Maisie, "She would." Aunt Maisie dismissed Sarah with a wave of her well-manicured claw, because she didn't find Sarah exciting. "I always think Sarah is too brown."

"She can't help it," I protested, "She and mummy have that type of skin. It tans easily."

"They look like foreigners," she refused to be placated, "Like Americans. And your mother's clothes are too young for her."

I laughed because mummy had made a conscious effort to dress properly before her visit. When she had returned from her second honeymoon she had brought her first ever pair of jeans with her.

"I have reached a milestone in my life," she had announced marching into the sitting-room and giving us a twirl. "Now all I need are a pair of DMs and a denim shirt."

The laughable thing was that when she found me altering a skirt later that day she had said, "Helen I really think that skirt is short enough. You must remember you are twenty-four not sixteen. You can't wear fool clothes at your age."

After dinner Aunt Maisie played the piano. My great-aunt was a very accomplished woman. She tore through a Mozart concerto in A major while I dozed and drank port and wondered if she would ever stop so I could retire to bed. I was exhausted after the previous night's events and the drive to Donegal with my parents. But poor Aunt Maisie was starved for company and I was only a young thing. Another late night would do me no harm.

Aunt Maisie stopped playing suddenly and joined me and the port.

"Pale little face," she said abstractedly. "Go to bed, Helen. You make me feel old looking at you. Sleep well and tomorrow we will pull blackberries in the back lane. Donegal has the best blackberries in the world."

I did not need to be told twice.

"Night night, aunty." I stooped to kiss her black head. Some said she dyed her hair with the best blackberries in the world. That must be one of the worst things about being childless I thought. No one to kiss you goodnight.

Now, tired or not I will never be much of a sleeper. And never in a strange bed. I left my windows open and listened to the comforting whispers of the trees in the garden. And thought beautiful thoughts about butterflies and sunlit meadows and the sort of things that send one to sleep. I did eventually doze over because I was wakened about midnight. Surely I had heard something to wake me? I lay still in the high springy bed and tried to decide if it was ghosts or burglars. And who was in most danger, them or me. The ghosts in Aunt Maisie's house were harmless, and usually I couldn't see them; but an innocent burglar? How would he survive her?

I lay on in the bed and waited for something to happen. I had not long to wait.

Aunt Maisie's head appeared at my bedroom window. I was on the first floor. Had she climbed the creeper? Afraid to disturb her in case she fell, I lay in bed fascinated. She was washing the window, singing "We Plough the Fields and Scatter."

The window being ajar Aunt Maisie climbed nimbly into my room and began to wash the inside of the glass.

"Aunt Maisie," I said loudly, "Aunt Maisie, what are you doing?'

She had the grace to jump. "Dammit, Helen darling," she came over and sat herself on the edge of my bed. "I didn't want to wake you," a bit breathless, but she was over eighty.

"Big full moon, dirty windows." Her eyes suspiciously bright, her breath suspiciously sweet. Gin.

"Couldn't you sleep?" I asked sympathetically playing for time. Give her five minutes and she would forget about washing windows by moonlight.

She shrugged. "Plenty of time to sleep when I'm dead, darling."

"Look," I said firmly, taking control of the situation. "Look, if you would like to go and get ready for bed I'll nip downstairs and heat you a mug of Horlicks."

"Horlicks." She sniffed her contempt. "Only old people drink Horlicks, Helen," but obediently she followed me out of my room and across the landing into her own. A Thirties-style silk nighty sprawled wantonly across the bedspread of her vast double bed. No spartan spinster single bed for my aunt. Only the best of voluptuous luxury. I handed her her nighty and said severely;

"I want you changed by the time I get back. Understood?" and before she had time to get stroppy I left her to it.

When I reappeared with the Horlicks and my smile carefully hidden she was in bed, embroidered pillows piled behind her head.

"My face-cream, Helen please," imperious now that she had been bullied into bed. I handed her her Horlicks first, supervised while she sipped it contemptuously then fetched the face-cream. It was better stuff than even Sarah used. The sort that cost more than a week's dole cheque. I carried it over to her with reverence. She slapped it on her face and neck with a glorious frivolousness commenting, "This is the type of cream your mother should be putting on before bed too. But you can't tell middle-aged women anything these days. They always think they know everything. No thanks in them."

I choked back a laugh. Mummy would not be pleased to hear herself described as middle-aged.

"I shan't sleep, you know," she said petulantly.

"Yes you will," I said firmly. "Don't let me hear another word out of you."

She was making faces at the Horlicks and reaching for her cigarettes as I shut the bedroom door. I was sure that if I had opened it again I would have witnessed her throwing the Horlicks out of her bedroom window.

Damn the old girl anyway. I was wide awake now. Something I could never do was wake out of sleep and doze back over again. I would have to read now for hours. So I settled down with Mary Wesley's *Jumping the Queue* which Aunt Maisie had presented me with earlier and commanded me to read.

"I think you will enjoy her," she had said.

I was enjoying her and sniggering at the naughty bits. Typical of Aunt Maisie to be reading such a sexy book.

Then I smelt something.

Imagination?

No. Smoke.

As soon as I smelt it I heard her thin reedy voice, "Helen, Helen," panic.

I leapt from the bed and bounded across the hall landing into her room. It was thick with smoke.

Pitifully, like Canute ordering back the sea, she was trying to beat out the fire. Her bed was ablaze and she was choking in the great belches of smoke spewing from it. Nothing short of a miracle or a fire engine was going to put out that fire.

"Come out, you fool," I yelled pulling at her arm.

But no. Aunt Maisie was determined to burn with the bed. What a stubborn old puss she was.

"My bed, my bed," she wailed in the smoke-filled furnace beating at the flames with thin old hands.

Vitamin deficiencies or no vitamin deficiencies I ripped at a brocade curtain attached to a window at the far end of the room where the fire hadn't reached. The brocade was rotten with age and came away easily in my hand. Without thinking I threw the brocade over my mad aunt's head and dragged her from the room kicking and spitting and swearing like a wild thing. Something literary seized me and I thought, eyes like hollows of madness, hair like mouldy hay.

I just had to get her out of the house, short of throwing her out of the window. I knew instinctively that if I let go, she would race back into the furnace. Her bedroom opened out to the top of the stairs. In desperation I rolled her down them. I knew I hadn't killed her when half-way down she began screaming a tirade of abuse in my direction. Such language! French face-cream indeed. She swore better than any agricultural student I knew.

Anyway she wasn't the type to take a heart attack from shock. Multiple fracture and suffocation in a brocade curtain perhaps but never a heart attack from shock. Not my aunt.

The roll down the stairs had brought her to her senses.

"Let me out, let me out, I say," she was shouting when I reached her at the bottom of the stairs. "Let me out, Helen; I've got to save my tea-set."

Aunt Maisie had a tea-set that meant the world to her. She had given it to me once when she thought I was on the verge of matrimony to a man she approved of. When my romance fell through I had given it back to her. It was a hideous grotesque monstrosity, but as age accentuates sentiment and she had been given it sixty-five years before she thought more of the tea-set than she did of herself or of me.

She was completely mad to rescue it of course, but I was madder for helping her. As the top storey of the house burned she and I ran in and out of the parlour rescuing the tea-set.

The roof was collapsing as I watched her exit carrying her leopard-skin coat and hat. I threw some other knick-knacks of hers out through the garden window on to the lawn: an embroidered cushion, a photograph of my grandfather with whom she had been in love, a bottle of gin and a heavy bronze statue of a naked boy. I followed the naked boy out of the window and on to the lawn. Aunt Maisie was sitting beneath the silver tree counting her tea-set. She appeared unconcerned that her house of eighty years was dying in front of her.

I took a tiny swig at the bottle of gin and passed it to her.

"Aunt Maisie," I said, "Aunt Maisie, were you smoking in bed?"

CHAPTER SIX

Great-aunt Maisie came to live with us after she burnt her house down. We all said it was a temporary measure; we all knew it was forever. Her fortune had stuffed the mattress of the big double bed. No wonder she had beaten at the fire so frantically when her bed took light.

"OK," I teased. "Why didn't you keep the money in the bank? Was the bank manager Catholic? Didn't you trust him?"

"No," she answered, "He wasn't Catholic. He was worse. He was Methodist, a clean Methodist. I can't trust a man who is too clean to be wholesome."

Mummy and daddy applied for planning permission for their bungalow immediately.

And Huge phoned me. He wanted to invite me to dinner. I had never had a first date to dinner before. I was flattered. He had a very manly voice on the telephone, like the hero of a romantic novel. I accepted.

Dinner! Even Laura was impressed.

"Huge is a real man," I told her with the faintest flutter of feminine excitement. It had been so long since I had a real man I had almost forgotten that flutter. I often fancied the hero or the villain of the novels I read but a hero in a book was no substitute for the real thing.

"We'll keep Aunt Maisie and mummy and daddy locked up until you leave," she advised, "No point in spoiling your chances with a real man."

I was tempted to suggest she join Aunt Maisie, mummy and daddy in the locked room. She was more dangerous than they could ever be.

I really was in a dither of excitement. I fed the dogs twice and forgot to bring in the washing when it started to rain. And I was still deciding what to wear when a big flashy white car pulled up outside the front door.

"Damn," I thought, would it be the Miss Selfridge via Oxfam or the Laura Ashley via Age Concern? I looked like a tart in the Miss Selfridge, but I looked like a virgin in the Laura Ashley. I chose the Miss Selfridge. No point in giving Huge the wrong impression at the start.

Making for the stairs, meeting Aunt Maisie heading for the front door too.

"I've been watching him from the sitting-room window," she exclaimed loudly. "Don't go out with him Helen; he's a pansy. I saw him looking at himself before he got out of the car."

I didn't knock her over though I was tempted. Instead I swept past her and wrenched open the front door. Huge hadn't even time to knock. Behind me I heard Aunt Maisie's "too clean to be wholesome..."

"Let's go," I smiled up at him. He was such perfect fodder for a romantic novel, a perfect male model for Sarah's magazines. He had a perfect car with electric windows and a sun-roof and no furry dice.

My evening wasn't boring at all. We went to a place in Belfast which Aunt Maisie would have said smelled of New Money. Remedial Mozart in the background and a very grand waiter, grander than Aunt Maisie or Prince Charles. He and Huge enacted the sacrament of wine-tasting. Huge congratulated him on the salmon but sent his steak and mine straight back to the kitchens because he judged them overcooked. I was sure the waiter knew my dress came from Oxfam. Huge talked while I ate; then Huge ate while I drank. I tried hard to remember his name. Maybe he hadn't told me.

After a skinny piece of cheesecake and a slimline cheeseboard Huge suggested we go back to his place for coffee. Where was his place I wondered. He had probably told me during dinner when I was eating and not listening. Warning bells sounded when he said "my place." "Work or walk" ricocheted in my head with "One organ not his brain."

"No," I said unsteadily, "I don't think that's a very good idea."

I'd never felt embarrassed before, refusing.

But then I'd never got to grips with a real man before. He made me feel young. He didn't question. He suggested we go home. In the car, still embarrassed, I decided that I had lost my confidence. Since I had been so ill a year ago I found it hard to get the balance right.

Yet Huge, all-powerful in the driving seat beside me, didn't appear to notice. Perhaps it was my imagination. I began to chat, cautious at first, then comfortably.

By the time we got back to Derryrose I had scrambled over the confidence ditch. It felt stupid to invite him into my house when I had refused to go into his.

"Thank you," I said politely, "I had an enjoyable evening."

He smiled. Perfect teeth.

"I enjoyed it too, Helen."

This was the point where the hero kisses the girl in all decent novels. Accordingly I puckered up and gave him the standard, sidelong "kiss-me" look.

But Huge didn't kiss me.

So I got out of the flashy car and went round the side of the house and in through the back door. I wasn't sure if the evening had been a success.

Aunt Maisie was waiting up for me. She had taken Daisy's room after the fire because she said it was the prettiest. It also connected with mine through an adjoining door. I suppose it had been a dressing-room in the past.

"You didn't kiss him." She was sitting on my window seat smoking out the window.

"Were you spying on me?" I was glad to take off my skyscraper black heels.

"Of course, with Laura and Daisy. Your mother and Sarah were probably watching from another window. But we were very subtle; we hid behind the curtains when his bus drove up."

"The car is rather flash," I admitted thinking of Aunt Maisie's Mini, a relic saved from the fire.

"Helen, dear, what do you have in common with that dreadful man? You are home much too early to be up to anything interesting."

"We both like rare steak," I said flippantly, "and red wine. Don't you think he looks like the hero of a romantic novel?"

"No, I think he looks like a crashing bore."

Mummy insisted we attend church next morning. Even Laura who usually volunteered to make the dinner. Even Aunt Maisie who was a sacrilegious old witch. The week before some blow-in family had dared sit in our pew. It wasn't going to happen again. We would all be in the pew by ten to twelve, a united family front, to show the blow-ins who was boss.

Since Reverend Robinson had been called to our church the congregation had swollen at a shocking rate. Blow-ins blew in every week now, upsetting the hitherto finely tuned seating arrangements. We Gordons had always sat in the pew at the back so, having been last in (we were always late), we could also be first out. We were always late because daddy stopped for the Sunday papers before and not after the service. We hid the *News of the World* under the driver's seat before we got out of the car.

"Scarlett will play up in the crèche," said Laura hopefully, clutching at straws. "It would hardly be fair on whoever is doing it."

In vain. Mummy was adamant. We were all going and that was that.

Acquired habits are hard to break. We marched to the front of the church while Rev Robinson said, "Good-morning everyone," and the congregation said, "Good-morning," back again. This was one of the reverend's tactics to make everyone feel involved. The blow-ins had blown into every other seat. Mummy tossed her crew cut to show she didn't care but her face was as red as Rev Robinson's hair. Only Aunt Maisie, resplendent in her leopard-skin coat and hat, enjoyed the attention.

Rev Robinson was dedicated to preaching the Word. So much to say, so little time to say it. So we sang only a couple of verses of each hymn, scratched the children's address, raced through the announcements and got to the sermon about twenty-five past twelve. I wondered a bit idly if ministers studied public speaking. Did they know that one's concentration lapsed after twenty minutes? I often felt that if I was a minister I would get the congregation to sing a hymn half-way through to wake them up a bit. By 12.55 Aunt Maisie was audibly gasping for a cigarette, daddy had passed his packet of Polo mints up and down the pew twice, and mummy was reading *Wider World*. In the choir only Sarah and Rachael the

minister's wife appeared to be listening. Rachael
looked faint. I suppose she had already heard the
sermon ten times before. I was sure Adam practised
on her. Some paint on her pale face would have done
her no harm, but I doubted that Adam would approve.
I knew Rachael obeyed her husband in everything.
Daddy said she was an example for us all.

"Doesn't Rachael Robinson look terrible?" I commented over dinner. "She has far too many children.
I didn't know that Presbyterians couldn't use
contraceptives."

"Rachael has ME," said Sarah. "When I was up at
the manse at the Sunday school teachers meeting she
told me."

"ME," said daddy. "I've had ME for years and never
a word of sympathy."

"Huh," snorted mummy. "Suddenly the country
is full of lazy brutes saying that they have ME." She
was just cross that she had had to walk to the front
of the church.

"Rachael is a big healthy girl," mummy continued.
"She should spend less time reading rubbish like *Wider
World* and listening to her conscience. There is an
article in it this month about marriage. And the
apostle Paul's opinions on it. He wasn't married
himself was he?" she demanded of Sarah who was
considered our biblical authority.

"I don't believe so," said Sarah.

"I guessed as much." Mummy was scathing,

"Rachael should take more exercise. She doesn't even cut her own lawn. I was talking to Eva Jackson in Wellworths. She says Johnboy cuts it for them. And she didn't even offer Johnboy a cup of tea when he had it finished."

"I always said Johnboy was a half-wit," said Laura as if this confirmed everything. "He couldn't take his eyes off you in church, Daisy. At his age he will be looking for a wife who can pull calves."

"Johnboy would be a lucky man if he got you," said daddy who was now three-quarters retired with Daisy in control on the farm. "If I got the chance again I would buy a woman who was willing to work."

Mummy didn't rise to the bait as was intended. "It's not ME you have," she said. "It's senile dementia."

Aunt Maisie had been very quiet since leaving church. Suddenly she chirped up, "Well, actually there was a man making eyes at me in church as well."

Silence. Then all together we said, "Who?"

"Of course I don't know his name." She was preening herself. "He was wearing a yellow tie. Hunting yellow."

Mummy groaned loudly, but daddy was delighted. "That was Bobby Lennox, smartest man in your country. He is the district master of the Orange lodge in this area, Aunt Maisie."

"He's an old fool," snapped mummy. "He organised the Twelfth in Bellaghy one year and the Catholics stoned us. He used to be a Free P but he defected because they wouldn't let him drink gin."

"Oh goody," said Aunty Maisie, "I thought he was awfully handsome."

"I suppose you made eyes back again at him?" I teased. "He's at least ten years younger than you, you know Aunty."

"Of course." How majestic Aunt Maisie looked. She really was a tonic. "If you can date plastic men in vulgar cars I can have an Orangeman toyboy. I assume," she asked suddenly, "that his wife is dead?"

"He doesn't have a wife," said mummy. "He's the oldest swinger in town."

Huge phoned me in the afternoon.

"Hello," I said, "How are you?" I felt vulnerable on the telephone, shy almost. I could not remember his name.

"Would you like to come to the theatre with me next week?" he asked. So last night's asexual date had been a success after all.

"What's on?" I didn't want to sound too keen.

"The Importance of Being Ernest."

"Oh, yes, yes!" I forgot to be cool, delightful, charming and unobtainable. "Yes, I would love to."

He made arrangements about collecting me, and hung up. Huge wasn't much of a telephone conversationalist. The strong silent type I told myself.

CHAPTER SEVEN

I n his own way Johnboy Jackson was a fast mover. That evening, after he noticed Daisy in church, he came courting to Derryrose. The Rabbit came with him, of course, for moral support. I could tell he had milked his cows before he came because there were tell-tale splashes still sticking to his ears. He was very well dressed, in wool trousers and a check shirt, and he reeked of aftershave, to conceal the smell of cows I suppose. Washing would have been easier.

If he hadn't been Johnboy Jackson and he hadn't been invading the privacy of a Derryrose Sunday evening he could have been almost presentable. As it was he wriggled silently in his chair in the dining-room and watched Daisy, who paid no attention to him. She was sticking a flower picture and it required all her attention.

The Rabbit was very excited about something. She too was wriggling on her chair. I had been writing at my novel before they appeared so I viewed them with the eyes of an author. An air of disquietude in both I decided. God, but they were irritating, leaping around there. Johnboy was on the horn now, shaking his leg alarmingly. If the Rabbit didn't stop bouncing on the sofa and shaking her head she would get a crick in her neck.

Her news burst forth.

"I met Ian Flemming at the Port last Sunday night," she announced. "Hasn't he become distinguished?"

"Fat," muttered Sarah.

"Well I won't bore you with the details, but to cut a long story short, he asked me to play at the mission. Of course I said I couldn't." She giggled behind her hand. Pathetic really.

"Oh Sandra," Daisy was genuinely upset. "And you play so beautifully."

Poor Daisy; if the Rabbit didn't play at the mission Daisy would have to.

"Oh, but he insisted. He said he had been waiting a long time for a girl like me. Those were his exact words: 'I've been waiting a long time for a girl like you, Sandra,' he said. What do you think he meant?"

"He's after you," said Sarah.

"Well Sarah," said the Rabbit blushing puce with pleasure, "that's just what mummy said when I told her: 'He must be after you, Sandra,' she said. But I'm sure she's wrong"—puce deepened to beetroot—"What would a lovely man like Ian Flemming see in me?"

"Hmm," said Sarah, as if to say, "I wonder too." I knew what she was frowning about. She was thinking, if Ian Flemming fancies Sandra the Rabbit Jackson, how could he ever have fancied me?

"You are too modest, Sandra," I said.

"Daisy." Johnboy had spoken at last. "Daisy, there's a rumour going round that you have built a sheep-dip. Would you show it to me?"

Daisy had designed our sheep-dip, and she and daddy had built it. What this meant was that Daisy carried the blocks and daddy built them. We had all assisted except Laura who was a mother and mummy who had menopause. Even Aunt Maisie was there though she didn't do much. She dressed like a land-girl, her shocking black hair tied back in a pink silk scarf. She cried when she broke a nail, and became a liability when she dropped a block on Daisy's toe because Daisy was the only person who was working. I suggested she would be better employed making us ten-o'clock tea and led her into the house protesting. We let her track her initials in the wet concrete to please her.

"Johnboy is looking well," I commented after he had left the dining-room, with Daisy to inspect the sheep-dip. "I think he is getting better-looking, Sandra."

"Yes," said Sandra with pleasure, "I think so too. I bought him those trousers in the sales in Belfast. But they make his legs itch. It must be the wool in them."

"He should wear a pair of nylon tights under them," I advised solemnly. "That would do the trick."

She wasn't sure if I was joking or not. Usually I didn't tease her but I hadn't had any fun since lunchtime, not since Aunt Maisie's new boyfriend.

"You know Johnny Paisley," I continued, "daddy's friend who is in the UDR? He always wears nylon tights when he goes on night patrol in the winter. He says there is nothing to beat the heat. Barely Black are the best."

Then Daisy came barging into the dining-room, very red in the face.

"Where is Johnboy?"

"Johnboy is just leaving," she announced loudly, "He's out in the car waiting for you, Sandra."

"What's this all about?" I demanded when we had said our goodbyes and the Rabbit had gone. "I was just starting to get some sport out of the Rabbit."

"He's a guttersnipe," she declared, "a horrid guttersnipe."

"Who? Johnboy Jackson?"

"Who else? That low-life had the nerve, he actually had the audacity to criticise my sheep-dip." She was almost weeping with vexation.

"What did he say?"

"He said there wasn't a straight line in it."

As a mother sees no ugliness in her plain child, Daisy could find no fault with her sheep-dip.

Gently I said, "But there are no straight lines in it, D."

But that wasn't the point. It was the principle of the thing that bothered her.

"It's not that I asked his opinion," she stormed. "It's not that I wanted to know what he thought."

Half an hour later Johnboy was back at Derryrose

with half a dozen eggs and a hangdog expression. He apologised beautifully in front of us all. It was unforgivable what he had said. He was disgusted with himself. He would understand if Daisy never wished to speak to him again. But he hoped she would. He hoped she would forgive him so much that she would come to the pictures with him the next night.

I only wish Laura had been there to hear it. She would never have called Johnboy Jackson a half-wit again. But she had taken the twins to visit Granny McBride with mummy and daddy.

Sarah and I gave him a standing ovation and Daisy was so overcome she kissed his cheek and agreed to go to the pictures with him. It was only after he had left and we were examining the eggs that she realised the rashness of her acceptance.

"What have I done?" she exclaimed in horror. "What have I let myself in for?"

"Well," said Sarah reasonably, "we have never had a man here before who apologised with half a dozen eggs. Usually it's half a dozen roses."

I was sitting waiting for Aunt Maisie. She had driven off in the Mini about five o'clock to buy cigarettes and it was now after ten and I was becoming concerned. Not worried exactly, but concerned.

"Aunt Maisie," I called softly when I heard her rattling about in her bedroom. She was smiling idiotically and I could smell gin the minute she wrenched open the adjoining door.

"I suppose you have been rendezvousing with

Bobby Lennox of the hunting-yellow tie," I teased.

"Yes," she said surprisingly, "I have."

Such a bit of excitement. Aunt Maisie had been speeding into Magherafelt to get her cigarettes and had been caught by the traffic police.

"There was a nasty little man pointing a hair-drier at me from behind a bush. I had no idea what he was up to. I certainly wasn't going to stop for him. A lot of weirdos in the country you know; you can't be too careful these days. It appears however he was a speed cop and he and his little friend chased me in their big squad car. Well I put my foot to the floor of Mini. Poor wee Mini, how could she compete? They caught us at the far side of Magherafelt. Darling, I was not pleased. They were such pompous and unpleasant men, and not a bit good-looking, as your mother would say. So cheeky. Could I read? one asked. 'Of course I can read young man,' I said. 'In most modern civilisations people are taught to read.'

"Then he stuck the hair-drier under my nose. 'Read that,' he said. I was doing seventy in a built-up zone, he says, which is utter fallacy. My Mini is 1972. How could it do seventy? What was I speeding for? he wanted to know.

"Nosy little man. He made me awfully cross. 'I'm having a baby,' I told him. 'I'm on the way to the hospital.' They had no sense of humour. Ugly and dull. I'm sure no one ever married either of them. They wanted to know if my Mini was taxed and insured and if it was registered in the North. I said I didn't know myself. They quoted laws and bye-laws at me. It might as well have been passages of Scripture. They made me so cross. I slapped the one that was quoting. That shut him up. 'Madam,' said his friend. 'Madam, I am going to have to arrest you. You are breaking the peace.' So I slapped him too."

And then Bobby Lennox with the hunting-yellow tie drove up. And rescued the policemen. Daddy always said that Bobby Lennox could talk his way out of anything. "What's all this, then?" demanded Bobby Lennox. And Aunt Maisie who by her own admission had not dropped from the clouds yesterday burst into feminine crocodile tears. Bobby produced a spotless handkerchief and talked her out of a hefty fine. In fact he talked her into a caution. He ran rings round the policemen. They apologised to Aunt Maisie for distressing her. Aunt Maisie was gracious and accepted their apology. She fell madly in love with Bobby Lennox on the spot.

"My dear lady," said Bobby Lennox once the policemen had been dismissed. "What a dreadful ordeal for you. Permit me to buy you dinner by way of compensation."

"Bobby Lennox said that to you?" I was incredulous. "And bought you dinner?"

"Oh yes, I rather think he was taken with me. He is a delightful man, Helen, so interesting and so handsome. It is so difficult to find both in a man at the same time."

I ignored the dig. "And I suppose you had lots in

common," using her line of inquisition.

"Absolutely everything, darling." She sighed voluptuously. My spinster aunt, over eighty, sighing voluptuously. It was indecent. "We smoke the same brand of cigarette, we drink the same brand of gin. Your mother was right. He is fond of his gin. Then he played his gramophone and we danced in his living-room. He is a marvellous dancer."

"Oh, aunty," I was quite jealous. "You smart old tart. It's just as well the cops didn't catch you on the way home or they would have convicted you of drunken driving. You wouldn't have got out of that as easily, tears or no tears."

"Hee hee hee." Aunt Maisie was laughing. It was a curious sound. "That's what is so funny Helen. If they had breathalysed me when they did stop me there is no way Bobby could have talked me out of it. I had drunk six gins before I went for the cigarettes."

CHAPTER EIGHT

S o three of the Derryrose spinsters had found
themselves men. Daisy, to her surprise and
Laura's consternation, had had a great time with
Johnboy Jackson at the pictures. Laura and I waited
up to find out how she got on. They had gone to see
Dirty Dancing. Johnboy had bought popcorn, which
he had eaten loudly through the show.

"I suppose you sat in the double seats at the back?"
Laura was fascinated. "Helen, you always said farmers
were the worst for snogging during a movie."

"Certainly not," said Daisy, "There was none of
that nastiness. Johnboy and I sat six rows from the
front because I had forgotten my spectacles."

"Daisy," I said severely, "You don't wear glasses."
Poor Daisy. She was taking no chances with the
Rabbit's brother.

"I felt so mean," she explained, "because he was
on his best behaviour and he insisted on buying me
four different packets of sweets when I didn't eat any
of the popcorn. He can pack away an awful lot of
sweets for one so skinny." She said that wistfully I
thought.

Daisy like Laura ran to fat rapidly. Since she had

finished university in the summer her appetite had
escalated and Sarah and I had noticed how tight all
her clothes were getting. Her breasts had swollen as
large as Laura's and her bum was rotund as a football.
Tactfully we had decided not to broach the subject in
case it was just a phase she was going through.

"So you sat at the front and crunched popcorn?"

"And didn't snog?"

Daisy had been toasting herself soda bread. I suppose she thought that if she had resisted the popcorn
and most of the sweets she was allowed something to
eat before bed. I watched her load the soda bread
with jam and could visualise it sitting on her hips.

"No, we didn't snog. We watched the film. Johnboy
said that if he had been going to ravish me he wouldn't
have paid us into the pictures. He'd just have taken
me to a lay-by."

"Johnboy said that?" Laura looked disbelieving.
Laura was still convinced that Johnboy wasn't firing
on all four cylinders. But then she hadn't heard the
beauty of his apology last night.

"Oh yes! Johnboy can form sentences you know,
Laura."

She suddenly started to laugh. "He was so funny
at the pictures. There's a bit at the end of the film
where the hero comes striding back to claim his girl.
It was terribly romantic and I was trying to squeeze
out a tear. And Johnboy shouts, "'Come on, you boy,
you!'" really loudly. The whole picture house heard.
I had to laugh."

"Weren't you affronted?"

"Not at all. He had just got into the spirit of the thing."

"So you are prepared to go out with him again?" Laura, scandalised, was almost afraid to ask.

Daisy screwed up her nose. "I might," she conceded, "I know he is a bit of an eejit, but I haven't had as much fun on a date since I went out with Charlie Montgomery. And that's years ago."

Oh dear. I watched with horrid fascination while she consumed another piece of soda bread. Life was never simple. Charlie Montgomery was the first great love of Daisy's life. He had been her boyfriend at UCD. A B-category man, he had left her for our youngest sister Jennifer. Jennifer and he had got married shotgun in April, and their baby was due next month. It wasn't a subject that we discussed at Derryrose. We weren't an intimate family.

When Sarah came home from her night class I called her into my bedroom to relate to her the details of Daisy's date. But it wasn't really Daisy's date that I wanted to discuss. I used that as a smoke screen. It was Daisy. And Charlie Montgomery. Sarah was a feminist and she took night classes in car mechanics but she had a soft heart.

"I think I know why she is eating so much," I said. "Do you think that she is still upset that Charlie Montgomery married Jennifer?"

"Comforting herself?" Sarah looked worried. "There is very little that we can say to stop her, Helen.

Putting her on a diet won't increase her feelings of self-worth."

Sarah always spoke like that. As if she was an android. "She must feel unloved and insecure. I read that people who comfort-eat have a very low opinion of themselves."

"I thought myself that she was more assertive than she used to be. Maybe it's a cover. What do you suggest?"

I was feeling embarrassed, discussing all this personal detail. Much simpler to sweep it under the carpet. It is difficult to talk about feelings when you have not been encouraged to express yourself as a child. At Derryrose that was termed showing off. I still locked my bedroom door before I had a good cry.

Sarah sighed. "I really don't know," she confessed. "But I'm sure that Johnboy Jackson isn't the answer, no matter how much fun he was at the pictures. He sits in the car-park with Willie Simpson on Sunday nights in Magherafelt. Imagine Daisy going out with someone whose friend went to Special Care school."

We contemplated the shame.

"Maybe we are being judgemental," I said, though I secretly agreed with her. If Daisy was seen sitting in Magherafelt car-park in Johnboy's Maxi, mummy would drag her home by the ear. And if mummy didn't one of the rest of us would.

"I think we must make a particular effort to be kind to her," said Sarah. "I shall discuss it with mummy myself. And tell her to take her menopause out on somebody else. And Helen, I wish you wouldn't encourage her to frequent second-hand clothes shops. Mummy is so easily led. She will be drinking in pubs next."

Mummy had tentatively accompanied me on a charity-shop expedition to Belfast just after her honeymoon. She became hooked on second-hand clothes, boycotted Dunnes and refused now to pay more than a fiver for any outfit. Of course she told no one that she had sunk to scavenger level and we were all sworn to secrecy. Sarah still had hot flushes thinking about it. She was sure mummy was going to be caught out in a dress the minister's wife had given away.

Mummy had been playing-up badly since Aunt Maisie came to live with us. She had battered me with Scarlett's pram straps that morning because I hadn't washed the breakfast dishes when she told me to.

"It was a mistake to educate you," she had screamed at me and I had swallowed back a mad desire to laugh because she had two curling brushes sticking out from her head like antennae. Every morning she styled her crew cut to cover the hole her hair left at the back of her head. She kept the brushes in her hair to train it to sit back.

"Mummy," I had said. "There is no hot water. The range has gone out twice. I can't get it to light. The sticks are damp."

This was the latest economy drive at Derryrose. Now we left the sticks out in the rain so they were damp so they didn't burn away too fast. We were saving to build mummy and daddy their brown-and-white bungalow at the bottom of the drive. The sticks were too wet to catch light and though we were resigned to living without central heating I was convinced of impending massacre if we were to continue without hot water.

Mummy didn't apologise. That was a sign of weakness. Churchill had never apologised. She made me wash the dishes in cold water. And before I had time to run away and hide she presented me with the mop, the mop-bucket and instructions on kitchen-floor cleaning. There is no pleasing some people.

However, when Sarah and I broached the subject of Daisy's comfort-eating she was actually sympathetic.

"Poor Daisy," she said. "Always had a clinging nature. Look what happened that old witch Maisie when Kenneth Gordon didn't marry her."

This was one of the less dangerous skeletons in the family cupboard. My grandfather Kenneth had married Aunt Maisie's sister Sarah, though Aunt Maisie had loved him and nobody else. She fell in love once, my aunt, and forever. I am not convinced that she turned out the way she did because of thwarted love. I think she would have become an eccentric alcoholic anyway.

But mummy is a romantic so she didn't read Sarah's logical magazines and knew nothing of the psychology of self-worth. She preached the power of having a man. Hence her surprising enthusiasm concerning Johnboy Jackson's courting at Derryrose. At dinner-time she asked Daisy about her date. Daisy was a bit defensive. She must have reconsidered its apparent success.

"I did enjoy myself," she confessed. "But mummy you know yourself what sort of a reputation Johnboy Jackson has."

"Oh don't worry about that." Mummy was encouraging. "You can change him. Didn't your father run the country with the gather-ups of Magherafelt before I met him? Didn't you, Kenny?"

The planning permission for the bungalow had come through so she was speaking to daddy that day.

"Cecil Simpson was my friend," said daddy. "We used to dance together when we were full."

Mummy laughed. "That's Willie Simpson's father," she explained. "He was like an octopus in a car. I was too nice a girl to go home from dances with him."

Daisy wasn't convinced. "But you often say yourself you had no sense. Do you want to know what Johnboy said last night? He said you could always tell a woman's touch around a farmyard. He is only looking for a strapping girl to do his work for him."

"Of course, he isn't," soothed mummy. "Anyway you can pretend you will help him until he has the ring on your finger. Then you don't have to do a thing. Like I did with your father."

"He says that the life of a dairy farmer is very lonely." Daisy started to peel another potato. "Did you bake an apple tart this morning, Helen?"

"No," I told her. "I was too busy negotiating that foreign object, the mop-bucket."

"Dairy farming *is* lonely," continued Daisy. "And now I have to share a bedroom with Sarah I can't even have Sue in bed with me. Sarah thinks dogs carry disease. I wish Aunt Maisie would go off and live in sin with Bobby Lennox so I could have my room back again."

"She'll never marry him," I prophesied. "She's a confirmed spinster. I might be one of those myself, a confirmed spinster."

"Well," said daddy, "It seems there are more confirmed spinsters in this house than you Helen. You are all far too choosy. It is just as well that your mother wasn't choosy or she wouldn't have taken me. And look what she would have been missing."

We were making no progress with Daisy. Valiantly I said, "I like Johnboy, Daisy."

She was sceptical. "Really? I thought you agreed with Laura that he was a half-wit. He told me last night about your suggestion to stop him itching in his wool trousers."

"I was serious," I laughed, "And I have reconsidered my opinion of him dramatically since Sunday. He was always handicapped in my estimation by being Sandra's brother."

"What's wrong with him being a half-wit?" asked mummy suddenly. "I would get bored with your father if he wasn't a half-wit."

"Oh dear," mummy added when Daisy and daddy had pulled on their wellies and gone out the back door, "Oh dear. I never noticed that fat little bum before. We shall have to take some drastic action before she gets so fat that Johnboy Jackson is the only man who will look at her."

CHAPTER NINE

There was a terrible lot of talk at Derryrose about Ian Flemming's mission. And about going to it and about not going to it. None of us wanted to go. Even its entertainment prospect couldn't render it more appealing.

"I just hate it," said Laura, "when there isn't any politics to spice the preaching up a bit. Religion is so boring without Ian 'No Surrender' Paisley. Daddy and I went to a mission once, and they said that the Pope was the Antichrist and the mass was blasphemous. I love the way Ian stirs an audience."

"It's a congregation, not an audience," Sarah corrected her, "and Ian has no political aspirations. He has become a real Christian and I'm taking the Girls Brigade on Friday night to hear him."

You could depend on Sarah, a real religious professional. Personal opinion was made to take the back seat.

"We'll all have to go," added Daisy, "Ian has asked us personally."

For indeed, Ian, with the Rabbit in tow, had visited Derryrose the night Huge took me to *The Importance of Being Ernest*. Though I had missed their visit I had missed none of the details because we had talked of nothing else since. Ian had stayed two hours. The visit began with a Bible reading and ended with a prayer, and in between he ate two banana sandwiches made from the heel of the loaf and half a packet of custard creams which were 17p and on special offer in Wellworths. Sandra didn't speak a word the entire time but sat on his right-hand side on the sofa, dumb with rapture. When their toes touched as she recrossed her legs she blushed peony pink.

Laura thought it was love. "The spiritual kind, not the sexual."

"Ian needs us there," said Daisy, "in case no one else turns up. Tents are so draughty, worse than the milking-parlour.'

"Of course we'll go," said Laura, "I enjoyed Ian on Thursday night. And didn't he leave us a dozen religious tracts to read through? I gave one to Shaun this morning. My Shaun is so smart he can read with his eyes closed."

In the end we all went together on the first night. And joined the little old ladies in knitted berets and little old men in the suits they would be buried in. And sang the choruses, Ian and Sandra accompanying on guitar and piano respectively.

After welcoming us most warmly, Ian, with a deplorable lack of nerves, introduced the Salvation Singers. Middle-aged men mostly, cleaner versions of daddy. They sang a piece by FB Bailey who was, I think, my sheep lecturer at UCD. An alternative farming enterprise, perchance? One man gave his testimony. He had been a drug-crazed hippie in his youth. Now he was a small fat man in a brown suit like everyone else. They finished by singing "The Gentle Shepherd" also by FB Bailey which was very appropriate if FB Bailey was the man I thought he was.

Sandra seemed oblivious to all but Ian. She watched him with doglike devotion.

"She has done something to herself," Sarah muttered critically as we bent in prayer. The Salvation Singers in front of us were groaning "Amen" at the end of Ian's sentences so it was noisy enough to chat without being overheard.

"No," I muttered back again, "It's just that hat. Where did she get it?"

Regretfully I had interest in neither Sandra nor Ian. I was in a hot fantasy about Huge and our theatre date. I had kissed him firmly on the mouth in the car-park before we drove home. Having loved Richard Knight unsuccessfully had taught a hard lesson about fatal hesitation. Huge had been impressed. He had kissed me back with enthusiasm. But he hadn't suggested that we go back to his place. If I fancied a bit of rumpy-pumpy I could see that I was going to have to initiate it myself. Huge, once bitten, was in no rush to repeat a refusal.

"It's not the hat," Sarah whispered aggressively. "I think she is wearing make-up."

"At a mission? Never!" But inspecting the Rabbit

carefully, I could see that Sarah was right. There was something different about her.

"Love," I diagnosed. "The Rabbit is in love. I've seen that dopey look before."

I had worn that dopey look myself.

Ian preached the tried and tested formula, but he preached it with youthful enthusiasm. Hell and damnation combined with "Ye Must Be Born Again" (John 3: 16) always works well whether at a mission, a death-bed or a funeral. I could feel the flames of hell licking round my ankles. Glancing at the Rabbit I thought she looked ecstatic. She was having an experience. Sarah was also having an experience, not the same as the Rabbit. Daisy and Laura on my left were enjoying themselves enormously. Laura had pushed her hat on to the crown of her head like a cowboy in a saloon and was grinning at me.

Ian asked for anyone who felt the call of God to come to the front of the church. I wriggled with embarrassment in the awkward silence that followed.

"Someone in this place is being called by God tonight," thundered Ian. "Ye must be born again."

The Rabbit rose from the piano stool and walked to the front.

It was a beautiful moment.

"Hallelujah," said the Salvation Singers.

"So," said Daisy who had learned the intimate details from Johnboy, "So Sandra and Ian are now in love. The scales fell from Ian's eyes and before he got a good look at Sandra he had put on his rose-coloured spectacles. It's really sweet. Johnboy went to the mission last night. He says Ian preached magnificently. He is going to stick to hell and damnation all week."

"That's nice," I said vaguely. My nightmare was back. The first time in months. The same dream I had been having since I discovered boys.

I was to be married. Sometimes I was on the way to the church, wrapped in white. Sometimes it was the day before the wedding. Sometimes I knew the face I was to marry and sometimes I didn't.

But one thing was the same. Always. I was making a terrible mistake. The uncontrollable panic was the same in every dream. When I woke, sweating and crying, I could forget the cause but never the panic. I was always depressed after my nightmare.

"What's the matter, Helen?" Daisy interrupting my melancholia. We were in the garden selecting aesthetic potatoes for the harvest service at church. Without fail Sarah volunteered us for the vegetable contribution. Before the Friday night mission she would help Rachael Robinson organise the PWA and they would have a jolly evening of fellowship and organisation and decoration.

"I had my nightmare last night," I told her conversationally. Daisy and I had shared a room at college. She knew about the nightmare because she often had to wake me out of it.

"Oh dear," she frowned, "Who were you marrying

this time?" Daisy attached mysterious importance to the face I was going to marry.

"Huge," I said. "Poor Huge. Two dates and I'm trying to get away already." I hated to fuss about the nightmare but had to talk about it before I could forget.

"Huge and I are going to have a purely physical relationship," I said. "There is going to be none of this marrying nonsense. What do I have to be worrying about?"

Huge was the first man to come courting to Derryrose to be referred to by my parents as a man. On Thursday night when his swanky white car pulled up the drive, daddy, who had been in the garden, dashed into the house (odd) and had shouted up the stairs, "Helen, that man is here."

"I suppose you didn't sleep a wink afterwards," Daisy comforted.

"Of course not. And when I finally thought I was getting over to sleep about seven mummy came barging in to get me up to bake soda bread. Some sort of a notion she took. She didn't even say please."

People had begun to flock to Ian's mission. The woman standing in front of me at the post office had been there each evening. Ian hadn't altered his formula all week. Hell and damnation gives one such a cheap thrill.

"I trembled," the woman told her friend in the queue. "I trembled for my soul."

The Girls Brigade had gone and seventeen girls had walked to the front of the tent to be saved.

"It was wonderful," said the woman, "To see those girls go, and not a bit embarrassed. I would have gone myself but everybody would have thought I was silly-looking standing beside them."

I could hardly wait to get home to interrogate Sarah. It was a pity that missionaries took Saturday night off in preparation for the sabbath or Laura and I could have gone again. I was sure that if that woman in the post office got the chance again she would go to the front herself.

But I met Sandra as I left the post office. She looked radiant, Sandra the sunbeam for Jesus. I bet Sandra never had jilting-at-the-altar dreams. She was probably scheming right that moment how to propel Ian up the aisle. We had a chat by the post-box. Oh yes, she and Ian were having a relationship.

"Is it a marrying job, Sandra?" I teased her.

Yes, the shameless hussy replied seriously, it was a marrying job.

And Ian had agreed to preach on Sunday night in Reverend Robinson's church and she was going to sing "Fountains of Love" before he started.

"Ian and I have been rehearsing all week," she told me. "He wanted to play while I sang. It gives me such confidence to know that he's there. But Reverend Robinson prefers that Mrs Mulholland plays the organ. I think he's just being stubborn. Ian studied classical guitar you know."

"Sandra," I said approaching affection. "Sandra, I really am happy for you. That you and Ian have suddenly seen each other." I was idly wondering if I could write her into a book without her being recognised. She might even be flattered.

Sandra had the manners to look modest. "Yes Helen," she said, "Yes I'm a lucky, lucky girl."

Daisy and I went to church on Sunday night with Johnboy. We went with Johnboy for two reasons. One was to hear Sandra sing. The other was to save Daisy from him. He had asked her to come to church with him. That wasn't really the problem. If I was there he couldn't take her to Magherafelt car-park afterwards, which was the problem. Daisy might disgrace us all. Sarah and the willing pilgrims of the PWA had made a great job of decorating the church. Little wonder that Reverend Robinson hadn't let Ian play for Sandra. He might have knocked over an elaborate flower arrangement *en route* from the pulpit.

If Ian hadn't looked so pious I think he would have looked pompous in the pulpit. He swelled visibly with pride when he announced that Sandra would sing.

Sandra, in a new hat and long red wool coat, coughed self-consciously at the front of the church. She held a big file of music, the sort of thing I kept my notes in at UCD. When she opened her mouth to sing the organ accompanying her died.

Johnboy sniggered and nudged Daisy.

"Mr Flemming." Mrs Mulholland's voice was very

cool in the organ pit. Mrs Mulholland had been playing church organs since before the war. "Mr Flemming I think you have kicked the plug out. It's at the front of the pulpit. Kindly kick it back in again."

Ian, deflated somewhat, did as he was told. The organ roared to life and Sandra's voice soared. Johnboy sniggered again.

I don't know if Sandra's voice was trained. I don't think it would have mattered. She sang with more enthusiasm than skill, more confidence than ability.

"Hold hard," said Johnboy beginning to duck. "You haven't heard the high bit yet."

We survived the high bit. Sandra, perspiring gently in her Cossack coat, joined us once more in the pew. She sat beside me filled with evangelical grace, her eyes fixed only on Ian. And it must be said that as he preached his eyes were fixed only on her.

CHAPTER TEN

S arah was cross, cross, cross the week after the harvest thanksgiving service. On Friday morning she interrupted my quiet cup of tea and *Desert Island Discs* to demand I turn the wireless down.

"You are disgusting, Helen," she yelled above Tchaikovsky's *1812*. "Eating toast in bed. You have jam down the front of your pyjamas. No wonder you can't get a man to take you."

Sarah was a super soap star. I hid my smile at the spectacle she made, poised, hand on hip, head thrown back, nostrils dilated, lobbing obscenities. I had slept well; I had drunk my essential morning tea; I could enjoy her. It was *Dynasty* in the comfort of your own room. She had been stampeding through the house, banging doors and upsetting everyone for nearly a week now. And Derryrose wasn't a house where doors were slammed. They were treated with reverence. Otherwise they decomposed. Yesterday she had informed Daisy that she was disfigured. One of Daisy's breasts hangs lower than the other. That was out of order. I thought we were being extra kind to Daisy.

"What a rude cheeky girl Sarah is," I observed over afternoon tea. I wanted to console Daisy that having one breast hanging lower than the other wasn't abnormal. If someone had told me that when I was seventeen I would have killed myself. I knew nothing of sexual frustration at seventeen.

"She has been a hairpin since Ian Flemming fell in love with the Rabbit," said Daisy. "I overheard her telling Laura that the twins are the dirtiest infants she knew. The gospel according to Sarah Gordon, chapter and verse: 'A baby is not clean unless it smells of baby powder.'"

"And she told me to wash the mascara from under my eyes this morning after my date with Huge," I added. "The second commandment in the gospel according to Sarah: 'Only a dirty brute doesn't remove her make-up daily.' So under her supervision I scrubbed and scrubbed the skin under my eyes. The 'mascara' turned out to be black rings from sleepless nights."

"Not more wedding dreams?"

"No," I grinned. "No, just insomnia wondering when Huge is going to seduce me." Huge had taken me for a drink on Wednesday night. Aunt Maisie was probably having a more sexual time with Bobby Lennox of the hunting-yellow tie.

Laura joined us in the kitchen.

"You are missing the fun," she announced. "Mummy sent Sarah to hoover the sitting-room carpet and Sarah was so busy scolding that she dropped the cleaner on her toe. And she is bleeding like a pig. And her blood is red just like the rest of us. 'Get me a piece of lavatory paper,' she yells at mummy. Ladylike even when bleeding to death. And mummy throws a wobbly and screams, 'You are bleeding over my carpet.' You know she got the carpet when I got married, so she is still new-fangled with it.

"So Sarah does her martyr act and says, 'Don't worry about me mummy. It's only my little toe. I'm sure my balance won't be impaired if the toe bleeds away and falls off.'

"And mummy says, 'If it was an artery, Sarah, you would be dead by now.' She and Sarah are amazing. They keep on and on at each other because they both want to get the last word in first. When I left Sarah was reminding mummy of the time she got smacked for losing her silver bangle in the garden when she was one and a half. Sarah remembers those smacks like it was yesterday. And mummy is probably reminding her of all the times she got up to feed her in the middle of the night when she was a baby."

We laughed.

"But the best was last night," said Daisy, "And the row about the tape recorder."

Mummy had bought herself a tape recorder one Christmas to play Daniel O'Donnell tapes so she and daddy could dance to him in the kitchen. Like hairspray, and hand cream before it, the tape recorder became public property. Mummy, uncharacteristically, saw no cause for protest as Daniel now had a show on the television. So she could both look at and listen to him while dancing. In a fit of self-indulgence after a row with daddy she had bought herself a television which travelled periodically between the bedroom and the kitchen.

Like a pride of lions tearing Christians in imperial Rome her daughters fought for the tape recorder.

"Sarah had the machine in the downstairs bathroom," Daisy explained. "She was on her hands and knees cleaning between the floor tiles with a toothbrush. I asked her to move it into the hall while I was in the kitchen so I could hear it too."

Eating, I thought, but didn't say.

"No, she wouldn't move it. She threw a complete wobbly and started crying. She locked the bathroom door and shouted that she wasn't sharing it with me and she would not listen to my classical music. She has played the Belinda Carlyle tape so often it's bound to be ready to fall apart. And I could stamp my little foot as often as I liked I wasn't getting it."

For the record Daisy has never stamped her foot in her life.

"Sarah never realised that mummy was in the kitchen too, and mummy took some notion and decided to defend me and confiscated the tape recorder and no one is allowed it now."

"Sarah needs a man," said Laura. "It is wonderful how upset she is that Ian Flemming has got himself a girlfriend. She doesn't even like Ian any more. I must say that I have rather fancied him since I heard his blood, fire and fury at the mission."

"I don't think that it's Ian at all," said Daisy, "I

think it's just the fact that Ian and Sandra have got each other and she has no one."

That evening mummy and I were watching *The Quiet Man* for the thirty-seventh time in the sitting-room. *The Quiet Man* and *Gone with the Wind* are cult films in our house. Laura called her twins Scarlett and Shaun for her favourite characters. We had got to the bit where Shaun Thornton breaks the bedroom door down to get to Mary Kate.

"There will be no locks or bolts between us Mary Kate," when the roof shuddered above us and the lampshade rocked.

Someone was in the big attic. There are two attics in Derryrose. A small one where Laura went as a teenager to find herself, and a large one where we went to find anything that was lost. Boxes had been piled into the big attic for years. It was dangerous, the big attic, with too many memories crowding the one airspace. I never went there alone, I always found things I would rather forget; photographs of spot-ridden adolescence; boxes of Enid Blyton novels. Who was foolish enough to visit the big attic?

"I wonder who is wrecking upstairs?" Mummy was half-way down a bottle of stout, so engrossed in *The Quiet Man* she didn't care if the roof fell in round us. I decided to investigate.

Sarah was swearing when I joined her. She had lost the torch in the chaos of spilt jigsaw puzzles, bedspreads and wooden tennis rackets with broken strings.

"I set the damned thing down for thirty seconds and it disappears," she wailed. We found it eventually, wedged between a picture of the Mona Lisa and a box of UCD memorabilia.

"What are you looking for?" Why would anybody in their right mind visit this den?

"I'm looking for something," she was secretive in the thin light of the bulb above us.

"Can I help?" Daisy and I had decided to be specially kind to Sarah, since she was so traumatically manless. I wouldn't have been surprised to discover that Sarah and Daisy had a similar pact concerning me.

"Look," said Sarah adroitly changing the subject, "Look at the padded cards daddy used to send mummy."

Daddy had a formula for Christmas, birthday, and valentine cards. It hadn't changed in thirty years. There was always a picture of red roses on the front. In the beginning the cards were A4 size, boxed and padded with romantic messages inside, now he sent Sarah or me into the shop to buy them for him.

"And here are the acceptances sent about their wedding." She handed me a box.

"Yes, indeed," I said, "But what are you looking for?"

"Something."

Rather than leave her I feigned interest in the box I had carried home from UCD. I hated to rummage through my UCD past, it reminded me of the Name That Must Not Be Spoken. What an unfortunate box

to choose. I had forgotten all the fun bloody Richard
and I used to have, which was a pity. It is boring to
remember only the bad times.

The messages exchanged on 29 November in
Physics concerned a disco the following evening in
Lansdowne Rugby Club. At that time I was being
pursued by a red-hot country boy called Eoin who
crunched his Polo mints when he sat beside me. I
had composed a begging letter which concluded:

> *I entreat your finer feelings, Richard. If you don't*
> *accompany me to Lansdowne tomorrow night I shall*
> *be unprotected and open to the mercy of Eoin, a*
> *fate more frightening than rape.*

In a moment of weakness I had shifted Eoin and
now he wouldn't take no for an answer.
Richard had replied:

> *Rest your little vacuum, fair damsel; Sir R will not*
> *desert you. But your safety can only be insured by*
> *the donation of some liquor on your account to me.*
> *Your ever loyal, trustworthy, diligent, and more*
> *importantly thirsty servant,*
> *Sir R.*

Richard loathed Ag discos and could face them
only after strong drink. In a flow of artistic licence he
had then dismembered his folder to send me another
missive:

*Indeed your noble Lord may be so overcome by the
evils of alcohol that the skiving guttersnipe might
steal you away without my knowing.*

"Why are you laughing?" Sarah demanded
severely. Apparently the sanctity of the big attic was
not to be desecrated with laughter.

"I had forgotten the good times," I said.

Sarah's mission was ended. She had found her
quarry in her hockey bag, cunningly concealed
beneath four other hockey bags. We had all played
hockey at school though I don't remember any of us
enjoying the game. It was the botheration of carrying
the hockey bag along with a school-bag that I detested.
Daisy was particularly afflicted because she carried a
viola as well. One morning she was late and Laura
and I watched her from the bus galloping awkwardly
along the road, her Rainey scarf flapping, duffel coat
fanned behind her, school-bag, hockey bag, and viola
case banging against her legs. We watched with
detached interest. We didn't care if she missed the
bus and had to walk three miles into Magherafelt.
She wouldn't lie in her bed as long the next morning.

Daisy made it to the bus.

"Get on girl," the bus driver roared at her. He was
a nasty little man with no hair and pink eyes. Mummy
said he had driven buses when she was at school and
he had terrorised her too.

The final spurt up the steps finished Daisy. Victim
of an artistic stomach she set her school-bag, hockey

bag, and viola case carefully on the front seat, then
vomited up her breakfast, wildly, over the floor.

A Catholic girl on the seat behind us tapped Laura
on the shoulder.

"Is that your little sister?" she asked sympathetically.

"No," said Laura. "She is not my sister." United we
stand, divided we fall.

Sarah was holding a card in her hand. Holding it
as if it would bite her at any minute.

"What's that, Sarah?"

Wordlessly she handed it to me. It was from Ian,
neatly dated, neatly written, clean. I thought fleetingly
of Richard's dog-printed hieroglyphics.

"Read," she commanded.

*My Love, it is I again. The days are beginning to
become harder to bear without you. You fill my
heart with joy at your very thought, but like the
tides the waves of joy slip back out to sea, leaving
a beach of sadness. The lone figure standing by the
water's edge looking longingly out to the horizon,
waiting...*

I handed it back to her feeling faintly nauseous. I
didn't want to be reading this stuff, dancing on a
grave.

"When did he send that to you?" Small talk to kill
intimacy.

"He was in America for a month once when we

were engaged. I missed him awfully. I kept a diary to prove to myself I could cope without him."

My stomach churned.

"I'm going to destroy it," she explained. "It isn't right to keep it now when he belongs to Sandra."

"But it's only sentimental rubbish," I protested, "Daisy has memorabilia still of her reign with Charlie Montgomery. You will want to read it in twenty years. It will give you a laugh."

She was shocked by such callous chat. "You forget I loved Ian once," as if she was the only girl to ever love and lose. And it wasn't that she had a broken heart. She had dumped him.

"Mmm," I said, "I dare say Daisy wouldn't have anything as outrageous as that. Charlie Montgomery isn't the type to think such things let alone commit them to paper."

"I'm sure he tells his wife them." Sarah had retreated into her high tower, and sounded huffed.

I laughed. "Tell Jennifer about beaches and tides of longing? Are you mad? She would have him institutionalised."

Our sister Jennifer was a tough nut. Too tough to appreciate beaches and tides of longing.

"Well," said Sarah, determined to have the last word. "She will have to change her ways when the baby is born. She can't stay tough for ever."

CHAPTER ELEVEN

Jennifer's son, Frederick George, was born on 1 November. The baby, her first, was delivered by his great-grandfather. Frederick's father, his grandfather and his Uncle George were hunting at the time. Jennifer is the only Montgomery woman.

She telephoned home about 12 o'clock. It was Wednesday, shopping day at Derryrose, and I was alone in the house. Everyone else was in Wellworths with mummy throwing things into the shopping trolley, hoping she would pay for them. I always stayed home on Wednesdays. It was one of the few times I got peace to write. So I was furious when I heard the telephone shrieking in the hall.

"I bet this is a wrong number," I swore, throwing down my Biro and jumping to my feet. I had been trapped in a snowstorm with my heroine. She and the hero had just begun to get passionate beside a roaring fire in a log-cabin in the mountains. My imagination had left dreary November outside. I was frolicking with a Huge-like hero on a wolfskin rug.

"What?"

Having wrenched myself away from my book, I was in no mood to affect a telephone voice.

"Who is that?" It was Jennifer's voice, still familiar though no one had heard of her since her hasty wedding in April. She had left for Kinelvin and never come back.

"Jennifer." I was shocked. "What do you want?"

"Advice, Helen." Jennifer never beat around the bush. "I'm in labour. Is mummy about?"

"Labour," I repeated stupidly. I'm sure my face was a picture.

"Yes," impatiently, "I think that's what it is. I'm getting pains. I don't know how long between them. We forgot to wind the clock up last night and it has stopped. It must be labour. The baby was due in November."

"Where are you?" I asked stalling. I didn't want to tell her outright that mummy was in Wellworths. It would upset her.

"In Kinelvin, Helen; where do you think? Go and call mummy for me, there's a good girl."

"Mummy isn't here," I blurted out. "This is Wednesday, Jennifer. She's in Wellworths with everybody else. Even daddy went for the run. You know he likes to push the shopping trolley. It makes him feel important."

I waited for her to damn me to hell, and visit my iniquity upon my children, unto the third and fourth generation, like the second commandment.

She started to laugh. "Well, hell roast you anyway, Helen Gordon. Shopping day indeed. And I have only Charlie's grandfather here with me. Everybody else went hunting. Grandpa would be away too but his mare is lame."

"Can't he take you to hospital?" Standing in Derryrose, a mile from neighbours, three miles from the maternity wing of Magherafelt Hospital, it was a logical solution.

Jennifer laughed again. It wasn't nervous laughter. Jennifer had never laughed nervously in her life. She was a tough nut. "Helen, you fool, Kinelvin is at the arse end of nowhere. I would be dead by the end of the avenue if I got into the car with Grandpa. We'd get lost down a hole. No, Helen you are going to have to deliver the baby yourself."

"I beg your pardon?"

"I don't think it will be much longer now, Helen. These pains seem to be getting worse. Grandpa put the kettle on to boil on the Aga and he's away upstairs now to look for towels. I remember Scarlett sent the black maid for towels and hot water when Miss Melly was having her baby in *Gone with the Wind*."

"Jennifer," I said, "where exactly are you?"

"I'm lying on the kitchen table. It's the telephone. It's plugged in here. Grandpa is disappointed that the rat can't be born in my bed. He was telling me earlier that he and Charlie's dad and Charlie and George were all born there."

Grandpa must have returned because I heard her say, "It's Helen on the telephone, Grandpa. You remember her at my wedding. She was my bridesmaid and George took a powerful fancy to her."

Grandpa took the telephone. "Good afternoon, Helen," he said, "How do you do?" as if he had been greeting me at a garden party.

"Mr Montgomery," I replied, smiling in spite of myself, "I'm fine, thank you. I believe you are having a bit of excitement down there."

"Why yes, my dear," said the old boy, "hunting season started today. My mare is lame, damn her."

Jennifer took the telephone from him. "Grandpa has sulked all morning because Charlie wouldn't let him up on my horse. If I don't give birth to a boy he will never forgive me. He's gone off to get us a drink now."

Game for anything.

I said, "I shouldn't worry Jennifer. The whole process is quite natural. Like a ewe with a lamb. It just pops out in its own time. And didn't daddy deliver you in the back of the Morris?"

Daddy had been taking mummy to hospital to have her baby but the rebels had planted a bomb in Magherafelt that night. It exploded in the centre of the town and the police had everywhere cordoned off by the time my parents reached the outskirts. No one was allowed through, not even my pregnant mother.

Daddy argued in vain with the policeman. In the last desperate moments of pain mummy had lain down on the back seat of the Morris, and pushed Jennifer into the world. Daddy held the back door open, and a policeman called Clifford held her head at the other side of the car. Mummy said she never saw the point of modesty after that.

Jennifer laughed at the memory. "At least I don't have the half of Magherafelt barracks monitoring my performance. And Grandpa is a vet or he was one. He's just brought us in a bottle of port. He must have been hiding it. It's vintage."

"Jennifer." I was firm. "I don't think you or Grandpa should have anything to drink until after the baby is born. Jennifer, are you listening to me?"

"Oh bloody hell," I heard Jennifer swear, from a distance. She must have set the phone down.

"Jennifer," I bellowed into the receiver, "Jennifer lift the phone and talk to me." Mummy was probably admiring baby clothes in Wellworths that very minute.

Jennifer picked up the phone. She was panting. "Yugh, Helen," she said, "That must have been the waterbag." She gave a snort of pain. "This is awful. I'm sure one little drink would do me no harm. Grandpa has it poured."

"Tell him to set it on the Aga," I commanded. "Tell me," I added to distract her, "when did the pains start?"

"Oh ages ago. Last night."

"Did you tell Charlie?" Where was the useless shithawk when he was needed?

"Of course not."

"Why not?"

"Get real, Helen. He would have fussed and got excited. Him and his father and George. They are worse than a flock of mother hens. He might have driven me to the hospital and it's miles away. I would have been abandoned there at the start of the hunting. He spent the whole of last night cleaning his tack and polishing his boots."

She stopped talking and I heard the sounds of her agony in Kinelvin. As abruptly as it began it ceased and she resumed her conversation.

"Great country here, Helen. Huge ditches. You must come and visit. Grandpa's mare hasn't thrown anyone in years. And I haven't talked to a woman since I got married in April."

She stopped the chatter when the pains hit.

"Helen," she gasped, "These pains are different. Pushing pains."

"What's Grandpa doing?" I had to remain calm to keep her calm. If she panicked the whole thing would take a lot longer. It did with sheep anyway.

"He's holding my hand," she said, "And humming 'A Bicycle Built for Two.' I think the port is boiling over on the Aga. I can smell it."

"Don't mind the port," I soothed her. "Have you really seen nobody since April? Don't people visit each other in that god-forsaken hole?"

"Honestly." She moaned into the telephone before she remembered not to. It was gruesome, like a banshee. "Most of the country are afraid to come and see us in case they get bogged in the avenue and need a JCB to dig them out. It's a matter of honour, keeping the avenue open."

She moaned alarmingly. She was in no fit state to be making conversation. I told her about Johnboy Jackson sniffing round Daisy. That pleased her. Jennifer had always felt vaguely apologetic about marrying Daisy's first love.

"Oh, good," she said. "I always liked Johnboy Jackson. And he's a really good shift."

"What? When did you shift Johnboy Jackson?"

"Oh, centuries ago, at a birthday party. You were there too. And Daisy dropped the strap of her dungarees down the loo. It might have been Johnboy's house. We were playing Catchy Kissey, and he caught me and we kissed under an anorak. He had great potential, even then."

"We never played Catchy Kissey at the Jacksons," I protested, "We played Pass the Parcel, and Sandra always had a pretty birthday cake. She had a pink one once that looked like a fairy."

I wasn't convinced that Jennifer was listening to me. She was panting, short sharp pants; then she laughed a bit. I could hear snatches of "A Bicycle Built for Two" in the background.

"Grandpa wants to know if I would prefer 'The Last Rose of Summer,' Helen. You and he could harmonise if you want."

She gasped as another pain struck. I began to babble.

"Do you remember the time you slid down the tin roof at Jacksons and tore your bum on a nail? And Mrs Jackson wanted to clean the rust off your bum and you wouldn't let her, even though you could hardly sit down with the pain."

"Helen, Helen, it's coming."

"Scream," I encouraged her, "There is no one to hear you."

"Poor Grandpa," she muttered, "He's too old for this sort of thing. He's ninety-two. His wife died having a baby. The midwife wouldn't let him into the bedroom to her though she was screaming for him."

"That's the same bed he wanted you to have your baby in?" I was appalled.

"He has forgotten her now."

I heard our car pull up outside Derryrose. The silencer had a hole in it and made a noise like a stone breaker. In two minutes mummy would be here, in the house, on the telephone, talking to Jennifer. But I couldn't run outside and call her to hurry. I didn't dare leave the awfulness at the other end of the telephone. Jennifer had taken my advice and was screaming her head off. "The head is out," said Jennifer suddenly. "Grandpa says it's coming normally. It's being born. Oh Helen it's over; it's born."

She was breathing deeply, shuddering sighs. "Grandpa has it. Give it to me, Grandpa. Oh Helen, it's a boy."

Tears stung my eyes. It was the most beautiful moment in my life. My sister lying on a kitchen table had a son.

I heard mummy calling me. "Helen, where are

you? Are you on the phone? Who is ringing?"

She came into the hall carrying Scarlett. We always took the twins shopping, to make them smart. I held out my arms and took my niece. Handing mummy the telephone I said, "It's Jennifer. She's just had her baby."

Laura and Daisy were in the kitchen with daddy putting away the groceries. Neither of them looked at me when I walked in. Daddy was reading the paper.

"Jennifer has had her baby," I announced. "She is on the telephone."

Mummy was being reassuring.

"Of course he's normal, pet. All babies have big heads," she said. "No, don't cut the cord. It will shrivel away on its own. I don't think the iodine is a good idea no matter what Charlie's grandfather thinks. I know he's a vet but even so. What are you doing, Jennifer?"

"I'm having a drink. I think I deserve it." The roar came clearly from Kerry. "Boiled port."

"Where is Charlie's grandfather?"

"He is washing the rat. Is that what the hot water and towels are for?'

CHAPTER TWELVE

I decided to seduce Huge. It was Sarah's fault. Sarah and her feminist magazines. She thrust the article at me and obediently I read it. Apparently the New Man does not seduce in a passionate frenzy. He becomes friends with his woman first. I didn't want any of that nonsense. Lover was lover, friend was friend and never the twain should meet. I had learnt that lesson with Richard. So I decided to seduce Huge before it was too late.

Plan? There was no plan. We were going to Portstewart on Sunday afternoon. If and when the opportunity arose I was going to leap on him.

"I have decided to seduce Huge," I told Daisy and Laura at teatime. "On Sunday when we go to Portstewart."

"What are you going to Portstewart for?" Laura was puzzled. "This is November, Helen, not July. I don't understand you. The Bingo isn't even open let alone the Amusements."

"Oh Laura," said Daisy, "Think how romantic a deserted seaside town is in winter."

"Think how cold it will be," said Laura. "You are being silly, Helen. You'll die of hypothermia if you

go skinny-dipping in this weather. You will have to
be taken away in an ambulance."

"I read a book once," Daisy was dreamy, "where
the heroine screwed her lover beneath a beech tree in
winter, and the snowflakes melted on their naked
bodies."

Laura rolled her eyes. "You shouldn't believe all
you read in books. Why, may I ask, can't you seduce
him somewhere warm, Helen? Mick of the Shovel-
like Hands whom I went out with at UCD bought sex
manual magazines and they always stressed the
importance of atmosphere. Subdued lighting,
passionate music and a double bed to lie on."

"What about the heat of the moment?" I laughed.

Laura shuddered. "You mean aged seventeen in the
back seat of his father's car, with the windows steamed
up? And aching joints the next day. Not even Jennifer
sank that low, and look what happened to her."

Mummy and daddy had gone to Kinelvin to visit
their new grandson and his black sheep mother. If
God was good they would stay away until Christmas
and beyond.

"Well I have decided." I was firm. "If I leave it any
longer we will have become friends and he will love
me for my mind as well as my body, and before I
know it our relationship will be based on trust in and
respect for each other."

"That is what you are supposed to want."

"Not me," I smiled. "If I wanted a relationship
based on trust and respect I would date Daisy. I want

a frenzied fling with a B-type bachelor. I'm the woman every man wants. The bird with no strings attached."

Laura screwed up her nose.

"Laura," I said, "You are showing your age. You never used to be a party pooper. You have become cynical and hard. You talk as if Huge had feelings."

"Cynical and hard," Laura laughed. "You brutal boot, Helen. I'm being practical. Do you remember the Rabbit running cross-country at school? She was never coordinated enough to be on a hockey team. Her arms froze one day and she had to go to hospital to be thawed out. It wasn't funny at the time. That will be you and Huge, frozen together, belly to belly. Great way to get to know each other."

Daisy's eyes and mouth made three circles on her face. "Helen you mustn't injure yourself before Bobby Lennox's birthday party. Aunt Maisie would never forgive you. She wants all of us to dance with him."

Bobby Lennox was seventy at the end of the month and Aunt Maisie was organising a surprise birthday party for him. I had dismissed the idea when she had first suggested it. "Madness," I had said. "The shock will give him a heart attack."

She had listened politely to my reasoning, nodded her head a number of times in sage agreement, then gone ahead and organised the entire thing the way she had originally planned.

"Mmm," I said, "and she is going to dance the legs off Johnboy Jackson and Huge, she told me. She has been practising in the football club with Bobby

Lennox. You know they go there every Saturday night. She has invited most of the football club to the party."

"Johnboy is fit for her," said Daisy. "She approves of him because he fixed the windscreen wipers on Mini. I don't think she likes Huge, Helen."

"No," I agreed, "she doesn't. She thinks he has no sense of humour. Of course he hasn't. And he is terrified of her. If he thought she was going to dance with him, he would spend the night hiding in the men's loo."

"And this is the man you want to seduce," Laura scoffed.

I didn't give the seduction much thought. In fact I didn't think about it at all until I was soaking in the bath on Saturday night. I was bored with sublimating my frustrations. The heroine of my novel was having a raunchy time. Why not therefore me? And Huge was clean and smelled nice and had pale gold curly hair on his arms.

I blamed women's magazines for polluting men's minds. For encouraging them to believe in equality. For making seduction a woman's prerogative. For making men's feelings fashionable. Men weren't men any more. They were human beings and it simply wasn't good enough.

Huge was a marvellous lover. He pressed all the right buttons. But afterwards, when I wanted him to roll over and go to sleep, he didn't. He hugged me and held me in his arms and whispered sweet nothings into my hair. Lying across his broad naked body I felt satisfied but non-communicative.

We had walked the strand at Portstewart. The beach was desolate and deserted. I pulled him on top of me and kissed him when we sat down at the far end. Message received and understood. He drove back to his house, carried me upstairs and ravished me. If only life had always been so simple. I blew a strand of hair out of my eyes and rubbed my head against his chest.

"Huge," I murmured, "I must go home."

He didn't want me to leave. His arms tightened round me. "I'll take you home tomorrow morning," he suggested. "Stay."

I shook my head against his chest. So he couldn't read my guilty face.

"I can't. I must go home." I never dreamed of spending the night with him.

His big car chewed up the miles between his house and mine. I relaxed and rested my hand on the top of his thigh. Too comfortable to make conversation. We kissed in the car at Derryrose but I didn't invite him in. Too late I thought. He held my face cupped in his hands and stared meaningfully into my eyes before he left. I wonder what he was hoping to find or to give.

I had half hoped my sisters would be waiting in my bedroom, expectant. They weren't. I poked my head round Aunt Maisie's door wanting her to talk to me. She was asleep. Derryrose was still, accusing; my subconscious screamed.

Next morning Huge sent me flowers. I was alone in the kitchen when Interflora arrived. Daisy was outdoors, Sarah at school, Laura in bed. I seemed to be having this affair by myself. Depressed, I read his card: "Last night was wonderful, darling," and arranged the roses.

When Daisy came indoors for lunch and saw the roses strategically positioned, where they couldn't be missed, she looked embarrassed.

"It went according to plan?"

"Yes."

"Did you enjoy yourself?"

"Yes."

Suddenly the whole seduction meant nothing.

"Yes," I repeated firmly. "Awesome."

"I didn't expect you to come home last night." She was setting the table, setting the knives and forks the wrong way round because she was left-handed and held her knife in her left hand. All of us, except Sarah, were left-handed but only Daisy ate arseways.

"You didn't expect me to stay, did you?"

Without meaning to I banged her plate on to the table and watched the chips leap across the checked cloth.

Blushing hugely Daisy replied, "I'm sorry; yes I did."

Fornication embarrasses Daisy. An incurable romantic, she persists in believing in love.

"I suppose you don't love him, Helen," in a small voice.

I chewed defiantly, swallowed and said, "No, I don't."

"Well, good for you," she said staring at my shameless roses. "I'm glad you did it. I only wish I had the guts."

"What?"

"'Thus conscience does make cowards of us all.' Shakespeare I think."

"Mummy and daddy sent a letter from Kinelvin this morning," I said brightly. "They don't know what to think of the house. Mummy wonders that any of them are alive the place is so dirty. She reckons it should be condemned as a hazard to public health. Mice in the bedrooms, fleas in the beds, TB in the walls. It would be a kindness to bulldoze the house away and build a brown-and-white bungalow in its place. Daddy spent the first evening washing every kitchen utensil mummy could find in Domestos with his bare hands."

I handed her the letter.

"Jennifer has even less interest in the rat than we prophesied. She was back in the saddle a week after Freddie was born. So mummy looks after him and she hunts."

"Jennifer always gets her own way," said Daisy wistfully, scanning mummy's letter. "She would drown Freddie and not think twice about it. I remember her drowning mongrel pups when we were small. I wish I had no morals and no manners and no conscience."

"A bit like myself," I offered. "The no morals and no conscience bits anyway. I'd like to think I had manners, breeding and sense."

Daisy didn't laugh as I had intended her to. "Not like you at all, Helen. I think you were very brave to seduce Huge."

Daisy was a very nice sister but I distrusted the intimacy she generated unintentionally. She would have been as embarrassed as me had I confided some deep secret thought to her.

Daisy frowned suddenly. "Helen," she said, "is there something you aren't telling me?" She was looking pointedly at my belly. My gaze followed hers and I pulled up my sweater to reveal a hot-water bottle belted round my waist.

"Can't cope without it," I confessed. "The same way you wear your woolly hat in bed. When I can't sleep at night I can tell what time it is by how cold the bottle has become. When I woke this morning it was still warm so I washed my hair in the water."

"It's not only my woolly hat." Daisy shuddered. "I wore my coat in bed last night too. I don't know how Sarah survives. No hot-water bottle, no bedsocks, and she always wears silk pyjamas in bed. I never take my vest off. And she gets down on her knees on the floorboards to say her prayers every night. I wait until I'm under the quilts before I even think of God."

"She is as hard as boot leather," I said, admiringly, "and she looks so fragile. Do you remember her wearing a Just 17 T-shirt as a dress at the Port on

Easter Monday one time years ago? She was going out with Ian Flemming at the time. And she had bare legs and white stilettos. We thought she looked gorgeous. I don't know how she took the cold. I was wearing cord trousers and an Aran jumper. She always cleaned the stilettos with Jif after she wore them. And they only cost a fiver."

"She hasn't worn them since white shoes became unfashionable," said Daisy. "She has them neatly paired at the back of her wardrobe along with her cream ankle boots and her black Moses sandals, waiting for the fashion to come round again."

I laughed. "She will wait a long time before Moses sandals are trendy. They were last fashionable when Jesus was crucified."

We both laughed. All tension and intimacy gone.

"Poor Sarah," sighed Daisy, shifting her sympathies from me to the unsuspecting Sarah. "Do you remember her deciding not to buy new clothes before she went to teacher training college for the first time. She wanted to check what students wore before she bought anything."

"It would have been no bad thing if you had done the same," I teased. "You looked like the Queen-Mother in some of those flowery dresses you used to wear at UCD."

Daisy shook her head. "Manners, breeding and sense," she said.

CHAPTER THIRTEEN

Aunt Maisie had Bobby's Birthday Party planned. Her demands were stamped on all actions taken, even the clothes each of us was to wear. She sent me back to my room twice when I was fitting on outfits for her, the first time because my skirt was too short, the second because my dress was too low cut.

"Helen dear," she fussed, "Your clothing is too provocative."

"But Auntie," I protested. "I'm supposed to be provocative at my age."

"Not at my Bobby's Birthday Party"—she was spinster firm—"with half the country coming. His sister will be there and you know what jumped-up pipsqueaks they are." Aunt Maisie abhorred anyone with money. She belonged to a different class—those who had it once but didn't have it any more.

"Doesn't Sarah have anything you could wear?" Aunt Maisie had no opinion of Sarah. Why did she want Sarah to be the role model for Bobby's Birthday Party?

"No," I replied, equally spinster firm. "Daisy and Laura have already bagged Sarah's Winter Collection." Daisy was to wear a wool skirt with an elasticated waistband; Laura was holding her ensemble together with nappy-pins.

"Does your mother have anything?"

"No. I have already looked. I suppose I can't go now?" hopefully. This was beyond a joke. Mummy and daddy had escaped the party by deciding to remain at Kinelvin. To drive the Montgomerys mad. Aunt Maisie's relief was rather obvious. I knew what she was thinking. Had mummy been there she would have spent the night concealing her bottle of stout and attempting to knock it back when she thought no one was looking. Bobby's sisters didn't drink. They were members of the PWA and exchanged recipes for gooseberry jam not gooseberry wine. Sarah and Bobby's sisters were to be the role models of Bobby's Birthday Party.

Finally Aunt Maisie allowed me to wear a skirt which stopped three quarters of an inch above the knee provided I wore flat shoes with it. She told me she wanted me to look dignified. She was convinced that Bobby's sisters would be impressed only if I was rat-ugly and asexual.

"Stop," she roared at Daisy, who was making sandwiches the morning of the party. "Why are you using margarine?"

Daisy was apologetic. I got the impression that Daisy's mind was elsewhere. Daisy was sent straight into Magherafelt to buy butter. There were to be no second-rate sandwiches at Bobby's Birthday Party. Aunt Maisie was not convinced that everyone, bar

Bobby's sisters, would be so drunk they would not
notice the standard of feeding. Our sandwich fillings
were glorious, Sunday-school-excursion style: Mars
Bar and apple, chicken and pineapple, and never the
whiff of a hard-boiled egg. Aunt Maisie supervised
but did not assist, which was a daddy thing to do.
Come back mummy, all is forgiven.

For daddy's fiftieth birthday mummy had had a
cake baked for him, with a naked woman stencilled
on the icing. I knew Aunt Maisie appreciated the
common touch but when I suggested the same for
Bobby she feigned disapproval.

"Certainly not," she snorted. She was having a
china replica of Bobby's Dobermann, Sheila, on the
top of the cake. Sheila was a promiscuous bitch with
a sour temper and a tendency to savage the
unsuspecting. Though she had been repeatedly
serviced by every mongrel in the neighbourhood he
was silly about her. Aunt Maisie, an adamant animal
hater, had attempted for Bobby's sake to make friends
but Sheila was having none of it. She would have
eaten Aunt Maisie's leg off had she ventured
unaccompanied into Bobby's house. Aunt Maisie
would have to mortgage her Mini if she spent any
more money. I knew we would be eating potatoes for
dinner for weeks to pay off this excess.

Then Daisy decided to take a course on the sunbed.

"I have my reasons," she said ominously when I
confronted her. It wasn't as if Daisy was going to tan
or, if she did, that anyone was going to see it. This

was November: one wore thermals not a bikini.

"Well, you must protect your eyes," I advised, surprised that Daisy, the blabbermouth, was harbouring a secret. But there was a change in Daisy, not noticeable to the external observer, glaringly obvious to me. She wasn't eating as much. I never mentioned it until she was discovered doing exercises in the dining-room. She was clad in the orange leggings I had worn when I did aerobics at UCD. Daisy had always affected scorn at my preoccupation with the body beautiful. She had watched me at aerobics once, firing Maltesers down on my head from the balcony at the sports centre. When Richard heard I was doing aerobics he had never gone near the sports centre again. The thought of me bouncing in the orange leggings embarrassed him. I only found the classes enjoyable when standing beside the one man who attended. He wore skin-tight cycling shorts and was well-hung.

Daisy smiled bravely at me. I smiled back. "What exercises do you do for your bum?"

I demonstrated the bum exercises for her. "Walking is the best exercise." I tried to walk three miles every day. Having a lover made me more conscious of fat bums and sagging bellies.

Daisy was using two tins of baked beans as weights. "I hope to graduate to the big tins of carrots by the end of the week," she said.

Once there had been a sale of tinned food in Wellworths. All the tins were 19p. Mummy had stocked up in preparation for when the bomb dropped she said. Although I sometimes fed Henry the beef stew when he had no dog food left, we weren't allowed to eat any of them, thank God. I would rather the bomb dropped on my head.

I don't think Daisy expected me to believe her excuse about being out of shape. But I didn't encourage her to confide the details.

Daisy returned from the sunbed untouched by the rays but for two panda burns round her eyes.

"What happened?" I had been engrossed in *A Room with a View*. It rivalled *The Quiet Man* and *Gone with the Wind* in my affections.

"Oh," said Daisy, "*A View with a Window*. Is it on the television? I was protecting my eyes," she explained. "I thought that if I put Vaseline on them they wouldn't burn. Don't you dare tell Johnboy."

Bobby's Birthday Party achieved a degree of success. We were well warned. Laura did not drink but behaved in a manner befitting a dignified matron. I did not say shit. Daisy did not snog Johnboy. It was boring. Aunt Maisie drank like a fish, as always. The more she drinks the straighter she stands and the more precisely she dances.

The birthday boy, resplendent in his hunting-yellow tie, ripped excitedly at his presents. In addition to the usual aftershaves, pens and pairs of socks he received a couple of very posh ties. One, a tasteful offering from the Gordon Girls, and one, a very expensive effort from a sister who had left the price tag on it to impress him.

Bobby's sisters formed a coterie in the corner of the room furthest from the bar. I recognised one of them, a mountainous lady, from whose bosoms I had once rebounded when I bumped into her leaving church. This woman was married to a hell-raising heavy drinker already in full swing at the bar. Her pious dignity slipped somewhat when she glanced towards him. He danced the legs off any woman who walked near him. He was rather dashing, I thought, when he whirled me round in an Old-Tyme waltz. At least he did not, like other men, complain that it pulled the legs out of him.

Mummy had a thing about our being able to dance. She had sent us to dancing classes as teenagers but never to a disco till we were sixteen. She didn't want us to get "reputations" she said.

The dancing classes were run by a brilliant Belfastie woman who always danced in a pair of bridal white satin shoes. She wore black eyeliner and rows of pink plastic beads and though we never discovered her name we all wanted to be like her.

"The boys have got it wrong again," we would mimic. There wasn't a "boy" under thirty. They were terrified of her.

Mummy and daddy had come to learn to jive. They fought so much it was funny. "No," daddy would roar, "You are doing it bloody wrong, you stupid woman." People would attend just to watch them.

"Bad habits!" The Belfastie woman would smack daddy's wrist. And during the interval when we were encouraged to buy a "mineral" she would take my parents in hand and bully the bad habits out of them. We never told anybody they were our parents. Daddy always calmed down after he had a drink at the end.

Daisy had taught Johnboy to jive and we all took turns with him. Huge refused to dance because he had never learned and he always rejected offers of instruction. I think Huge thought himself omnipotent. To be unable to dance would have shattered his illusions of himself. Richard had always danced but that was irrelevant.

Aunt Maisie spoke to us after the supper when we were making going-home noises and the band had restarted "The Old Rugged Cross" which must have been a great party favourite with the football club as most of them were on the floor singing to it. And waving their arms as if they were at a cup-final.

"You did a marvellous job, girls." She bestowed praise with a sense of her own importance. "But why was it Bobby's sister that got the sandwich with the hair in it?"

The heavy drinker had drunk himself silly by the time we were leaving. I watched two of Bobby's sisters drag him out to their car. They didn't look shocked or embarrassed as I had expected. Maybe there was more to Bobby's sisters than met the eye.

We left the Morris at the party for Aunt Maisie and travelled home in convoy in Huge's white elephant and Johnboy's blue Maxi. Huge refused my offer of a quick roll and tumble on my bed before going home. I suppose he didn't enjoy himself. But how could he? He had no sense of humour. That's why I was going out with him.

Daisy was very pleased with her night. And Johnboy Jackson never refused a bit of nookie.

I slept badly because my feet were cold. I had left my hot-water bottle in the Morris joyfully anticipating Huge being here to warm my cold bits. The plan had been to defrost the car windows with the water in the bottle when we were coming home. Mummy and daddy had taken Sarah's little car to Kinelvin and left us the Morris.

About five I rose to make a mug of Horlicks and to find myself a pair of thermal socks. To my intense amusement Daisy and Johnboy were still courting on the sofa in the sitting-room. Neither noticed me as I slipped past the open door to the kitchen where the kettle was. I had never credited Daisy with that much sex drive. She was not that type of girl. I hoped she wasn't going to do anything silly with Johnboy Jackson. The sitting-room was cold and damp, and the sofa narrow and hard.

"They must be fond," I said loudly, thinking of Huge. No doubt he had not intended to slight me with his refusal earlier on.

I remembered once pompously telling mummy, "I am never bored with myself; it's other people who bore me." Tonight, in the kitchen, as the kettle boiled, and my sister shifted, tonight I was bored with myself. God. I was too old for arrested adolescence. I would sneak outside and call Henry and take him to bed with me. Henry and I had always slept together but the night after he binged on the burnt bits of Daisy's birthday cake in September he had misbehaved over my favourite flannelette sheets. Immediate end to a happy and mutually beneficial allegiance. I threw the dirty brute out of the bed and banished him forever. He had sulked, man-like ever since.

"Henry, sweetheart," I coaxed him from the back-door step. "Stop huffing, Henry. I'm sorry I called you all those cheeky names. I know you would have got out of bed first if it hadn't been so cold."

I was almost tempted to offer him a left-over cucumber-and-prawn sandwich by way of bribery but forgiveness is one thing, foolishness quite another.

I had crawled sufficiently. Henry appeared and leapt unrestrainedly into my outstretched arms. We kissed and made up. I forgot about the Horlicks and my pending depression and carried the love-object to bed.

I had forgotten about Daisy, too, and her shocking behaviour on the sitting-room sofa. How unfortunate she had not forgotten so easily about me. Henry and I were cuddled together in the half dark of the pre-dawn. It is only dark if you have no one to share it with.

Daisy did not dither modestly at my door nor edge on tiptoe into my bedroom, suitable behaviour for pre-dawn soirées. She wrenched at my ancient door handle forgetting it pushes up not down and stage-whispered, "Helen, are you awake?"

"I am now," I muttered, trying, but not succeeding, to keep a peeved tone out of my voice. To sound peeved would have suggested jealousy.

"What time is it, Daisy?" I asked sweetly, not moving in the bed.

"Only half past five."

"And what were you doing to Johnboy until now?"

"Just a cuddle."

In farmer vocabulary "cuddle" could be anything from kissing to sex.

"It was awfully passionate," she added, "but my head got wedged once on the sofa. Anyway I have made a momentous decision." Her voice was smiling. My blood chilled in its pipes. I knew what she was going to say. She couldn't be serious. She wasn't lifting weights, taking sunbed sessions and eating less for that reason?

Yes, she was.

"When?" I asked releasing Henry and rolling over in the bed to watch her face.

"When I have lost a stone of weight, had five more sessions on the sunbed, streaked my hair, plucked my eyebrows, tinted my eyelashes, waxed my legs and grown my fingernails."

"Sooner than later then," I said.

CHAPTER FOURTEEN

Daisy continued lifting weights but the losing weight seemed to be causing difficulties. Much too sensible and self-indulgent for crash dieting she told me she was using a slow weight-reduction programme. Apparently this programme allowed chips and sausages. She wanted her night of passion to have happened by the New Year. I suggested that there should be no time-limit put on virginity; it was not a millstone round her neck or a horsehair shirt. It was not a punishment. Such arguments had no effect. She was determined to be rid of it for once and for all and to enter the new decade a New Woman.

"I'm trying to resist all temptations," she told me, watching as I hung white lights on the Christmas tree. The trees on Grafton Street always had white lights; coloured lights weren't fashionable any more.

Mummy and daddy were due back the next day. It was essential that we had Christmas organised before mummy returned and resumed control. There was going to be the father and mother of a row because the builders of the brown-and-white bungalow hadn't progressed a block further since my parents left for Kinelvin in November.

"What temptations?" I demanded irritably. I had the rotten lights arranged but they weren't working when they were switched on. Something loose or frayed. Something else as well as my nerves.

Daisy did not notice my display of temper. She couldn't distinguish between stress and self-expression.

"Food, Helen, and drink. I'm determined to get some weight off by my big night." She was drinking lemon tea. She thought there was a correlation between my drinking lemon tea and being stick-thin.

"Have you a plan?" The lights had, by the magic of Christmas, decided to work. Life could go on.

"Oh, yes."

"Well," I conceded grumpily, "let's hear it."

"You know that New Year's Eve is on a Sunday? Well Ian Flemming and Sandra are singing in church, at the watch-night service, and Sandra is staying the night at the Flemmings' house. And Mr and Mrs Jackson always spend the New Year with Mr Jackson's brother in Ballymoney." She smiled triumphantly. I had missed the point somewhere.

"So?"

"So the Jacksons' house is empty, silly. Johnboy and I will have the place to ourselves. Johnboy has offered to cook me a candlelight dinner that night. We were going to eat out but we can't now, it being Sunday and all that."

"You must remember to tell me what candlelight tastes like," I commented drily, wishing she would stop drinking tea and help me with the decorations. Sarah's primary-school class had made chains of coloured paper last year and they looked distinctly tacky beside my elegant white lights.

"So," said Daisy who had paused to consider my little joke and to smile with understanding. "So, then, during dinner I am going to suggest we spend the night together."

"You mean you haven't told him yet?" The chains were coming to pieces in my hands. Damn Merry Christmas anyway.

"No," anxiously. "Do you think I ought to?"

On New Year's Eve I decided to go to the watch-night service. Usually I went to the Rugby club and shook my stuff with the people I went to school with. I was looking forward to doing something different this year. Huge had suggested that he cook me dinner at his place. He wondered why I laughed at his suggestion and had only been slightly mollified when I explained that that was how Johnboy and Daisy intended breaking in the new decade. I asked him to accompany me to the watch-night service. "We could slip down to the Rugby club afterwards for a quick one to drink in the New Year."

He agreed eventually. I don't think Huge was much of a churchgoer; he couldn't appreciate the significance of God on a potential party night. If it hadn't fallen on a Sunday, I, doubtlessly, would have also preferred to end the year at his place—with the atmosphere switched on and the overhead lights switched off.

"And we could go back to your place afterwards if you like," I added. It felt as if he was doing me some massive favour, coming to church with me. Huge wasn't as malleable a man as I had hoped.

On New Year's Eve Daisy started to get ready to go out at lunchtime. Sarah and I discovered her ironing her underclothes in the scullery.

"What are you ironing your underclothes for?" I asked suppressing a shout of laughter. Sarah looked at me, amazed.

"Don't you iron yours, Helen?"

"No, never." The idea had never occurred to me.

"Sarah irons hers all the time," said Daisy defensively, "And her facecloth and towels and night clothes."

"Why?"

Sarah feigned impatience. "How can you expect a man to marry you, if you are such a slattern about housework?"

"So Daisy will only catch a husband if she can prove she will iron his underwear and boil the dishcloths?"

I was sure I remembered mummy saying once, "He won't notice the dust under the bed, provided you keep him happy between the sheets." Maybe it had been my imagination. "Daisy would need to start lifting her dirty knickers off the bedroom floor," sniffed Sarah.

Ian Flemming and the Rabbit had exchanged friendship rings for Christmas, whatever they were. Sarah said she didn't care what they exchanged but wasn't Sandra rather obvious the way she was rushing Ian towards the altar. Certainly Sandra had begun to display a cunning I had never credited her with before now.

"I ironed my nighty too," Daisy confided to me after Sarah had left. Sarah wasn't the type of girl you revealed amoral plans to.

"Are you wearing these?" I held a scrap of black lace delicately between finger and thumb. "Do you want a loan of my black lace bra to go with them? And I have a black lace suspender belt somewhere if you are feeling particularly daring."

Daisy glowed. "Yes, yes, please. I want to feel the part."

"I will lend them only provided you don't iron them."

At the last minute when I thought Huge and I were escaping off to church alone together mummy and daddy decided to join us. Perhaps they suspected my make-up a bit much for the service. Perhaps they genuinely felt the spirit move them. One minute they were watching Clive James on the television, the next mummy was throwing on her Sunday coat and daddy was poking in the back of the wardrobe with the lambing torch searching for his favourite red tie. Huge was mute with horror. I ensured he did not have to sit beside either of them.

Praying our way into the new decade I thought of Daisy and hoped she was now the whole woman she wished to be. I thought of Jennifer in Kinelvin. She was probably lying drunk somewhere. And I thought of myself.

"Forget the past; don't look back," the sermon had said. "What's done is done. Forget past mistakes, past sins and lost opportunities."

"Don't look back," I repeated to myself. "Don't look back."

Mummy gave Huge and me her blessing when I said we were going to run into the Rugby club to wish everybody a Happy New Year.

"There is no rush home." She smiled at Huge. Mummy was awfully silly when it came to men. She ate them for breakfast.

"Have you got a hairbrush with you?" asked daddy.

Huge and I skipped the festivities of the Rugby club and drove straight back to his place. He poured me a glass of port but didn't give me a chance to drink it. Next morning it was still on the mantelpiece above the empty fire, where I had set it before he swept me into his arms and on to his bed.

I knocked it back with a practised flick of the wrist, before joining him again in the bedroom.

"Don't look back," I thought fiercely.

Daisy was in my bed when Huge left me home.

"Daddy is doing the milking," Daisy muttered when I walked into the room. I had been hoping for a bit of privacy, just enough to compose my face and my thoughts before joining the family in the dining-room.

Daisy sat up in the bed. Her face was swollen with crying.

"Daisy," I was horrified. "Daisy, what happened? Was it awful?"

Johnboy's candlelight and garlic mushrooms had been delicious. Sandra's Turkey Cordon Bleu, sautéd aubergine slices and French beans with thyme had been delicious. Sarah's (for Sarah had made pudding) walnut chiffon pie had been delicious.

Daisy had brought a bottle of Frascati and Johnboy a bottle of Chianti.

"The wine went straight to my head, Helen," said Daisy. "I haven't eaten properly in a month and I was so nervous I kept slugging it back. I was legless."

"So?" I said not wanting to rush her but mad to get to the good bit. "What happened next?"

"He made us coffee," she said with maddening deliberation. "And then he turned up the stereo. It was playing Willie Nelson's *Love Songs* and we started to dance in the kitchen dining-room. Except it wasn't really dancing because he was taking my clothes off at the same time. I was pulling at his shirt and tie..."

"Tie?"

"Yes we were all dressed up. His hand was sliding up under my skirt to the top of your stockings and I was fumbling with the belt of his trousers but my hands wouldn't do what my head told them. He was kissing my collar bones and the top of my breasts..."

"And?"

"And then I felt really sick, and I threw up all round me."

"Over him?"

"No I don't think so. God! I hope not. I feel bad enough as it is. No, just on the floor. I had to dash to the bathroom. He held my head when I was being sick."

"Poor Daisy," I comforted. "What did Johnboy say? Was he really mad?" I could imagine what Huge would have done in the same circumstances. He would have cried.

"Johnboy didn't say anything. He was too busy laughing. Then he said, 'You never cease to amaze me, Daisy Gordon; you never cease to amaze me.' And when we were sure there was nothing left for me to throw up he took me to bed and undressed me and left me with a basin to throw up into if I felt the urge."

"And he went back to clean up," I finished for her. Johnboy was a star.

"Yes but that's not the end of the story, Helen. I was lying there feeling a complete dog and the door-bell went."

"Sandra?" I asked in horror.

"Worse. It was Willie Simpson and a whole gang of them just out of the Rugby club and rotten with drink. Who am I to speak? And the black bra was still lying on the kitchen floor. Johnboy brought it in for me. I think it is the end of my life, Helen."

The poor wee sad face poked out from the bedclothes. I laughed. I reckoned that either she laughed about it or she killed herself.

"No, sweetheart," I said. "This isn't the end of your life. It's just the beginning."

CHAPTER FIFTEEN

The Morris was done.

A fact of life that nothing lasts for ever.

But you never expect it of a car. And the Morris was an institution. Daddy had bought it and met mummy the same week. It was his little joke that when the Morris went, mummy was to pack her bags and go with it.

Mummy had been so twisted and cross over Christmas perhaps even she appreciated that time was running out, the end of an era approaching. Anyway, if she didn't run away, as she constantly threatened, Daisy and I had secretly planned our own escapes, each for our own reasons.

On Christmas Eve Daisy had risen at the crack of dawn, and clad in my orange leggings, she and daddy had sorted out the last of the lambs and loaded them into Johnboy Jackson's trailer to take them to Swatragh market. Daisy had asked Aunt Maisie to ask Bobby Lennox to ask his heavy-drinking brother-in-law for the big blue Mercedes van to pull the trailer. When Bobby's brother-in-law was not drinking or recovering from the effects of drink he drove the blue van for a building company.

I feel it necessary to add that Daisy didn't usually canvass the country sponging conveyance for her livestock. But Johnny Paisley, daddy's friend whom she usually paid as a taxi service, had taken some notion and gone to spend Christmas in Scotland with his girlfriend Maud Evans, a platinum blonde mother of four. Mummy, with vindictive cattiness, said Maud had never been blonde at school but mummy was only jealous because she had always thought that Johnny fancied her. She said that Johnny had been the Casanova of Magherafelt thirty years before and he had given her spins in his car at lunchtime round the tech car-park when she had been at school. He had never looked at Maud but Maud had never been a blonde then.

It had been mummy's unfortunate misconception, as a townie girl, that farmers were a great catch.

After thirty years of standing to attention by a boiling kettle and stewing teapot when her great catch came demanding tea and scone on the hour, mummy was leisurely repenting of her hasty race to the altar. She had never read the novel *Of Human Bondage* but when she observed me struggling through it she enquired whether the plot centred on a farmer's wife. This was perhaps unfair, because when daddy wanted coffee he generally made it himself.

Anyway Daisy and daddy loaded the lambs into the trailer and came back into the house for a bite of breakfast before the cold haul to Swatragh market. Bobby's brother-in-law had dropped round the blue

van the night before, with half a dozen ladders still
strapped to her. He refused payment provided daddy
drove him to the pub in Curran which was where he
intended depositing his holiday money.

"Got to get it spent before the wife gets her hands
on it," he had remarked cheerfully as he and daddy
pushed the Morris to the top of the drive to try and
jump-start her down the hill.

Daddy, admiring such rebellion and honoured to
be part of it, had stormed the sitting-room and bullied
Daisy and Sarah out into the black frost to push.
Laura and I had anticipated this turn of events and
were slyly hidden upstairs.

Daddy hadn't come home until after closing time
when he woke the house singing "The Green Grassy
Slopes of the Boyne." Mummy then woke the neighbourhood and the dead by yelling at him and depositing a pre-packed suitcase of clothes on his head out
of an upstairs window. Having allocated daddy
enough pocket-money for two pints, one for himself
and one for Bobby's brother-in-law and having
calculated that he should be back home about nine
she had packed the suitcase in a rage about ten o'clock.

"Awh, pet," he shouted up at her, "Don't be like
that. I had a bath this evening, and you know what
that means."

"By my reckoning," Daisy announced at breakfast,
"eight of those lambs are mine and the Île de France
ram that we are selling as well. The hornie ram is

yours daddy and the other three lambs."

"Really?" said mummy, since daddy was sucking on a piece of bacon too hungover to comment, "Really? Daisy. When did you decide this?"

"Of course they are mine." Daisy didn't acknowledge the dangerous tone; she didn't raise her head from her piece of dry toast. The slow weight-reduction programme was playing havoc with her temper. "They are out of a greyface ewe and an Île de France ram."

"Well," said mummy in the voice she used talking to Aunt Maisie, "I don't claim to know everything about sheep but I can't believe that the majority of those lambs belong to you."

"No," said Daisy, undeterred. "You are right. You don't know anything about sheep. I will take you out and show you them myself. They are certainly mine."

Mummy threw a bit of a wobbly. "I don't believe you, Daisy," she said. "I think you are lying. You don't know anything about sheep. Your father lambed those ewes in the spring when you were in Dublin. How would you know what lambs belong to them?"

So Daisy threw a wobbly. Daisy is usually exceptionally even-tempered but deprivation of food had made her highly strung and she was hurt to be branded a liar.

"I was in Dublin completing a bloody degree in agriculture, mother," she screamed, surprising us all. "A first-class degree in agriculture. I ought to bloody know the difference between a Suffolk ewe and a greyface. And all the greyface ewes on this farm belong to me."

She was asking for trouble.

"Right," she said sharply. "We are leaving. Come along daddy," and she swept doghouse daddy out ahead of her. I kept my head down and wished I was upstairs in the comparative safety of my room. I knew that even if Daisy had managed to side-step the hailstones I wasn't going to escape as lightly.

As children, sent to our rooms to await a beating, Daisy had always been the first to crack. She began squealing the minute she heard mummy's tread on the stairs. I had always stood firm and refused to submit to tears or pleadings and this had always antagonised mummy and she had always smacked me harder than Daisy. She had always smacked Laura with a shoe rather than her hand because Laura had the effrontery to laugh at her.

She was glaring at my serene expression. I could not help looking serene; it became me. A frightened humble face wasn't in my nature.

"So," said mummy, "Why have you been looking so sulky? And when did you last wash dishes? Do I have to do everything myself?"

I did not answer for two reasons. Firstly because she required no answer. And secondly, because it made her madder if you didn't answer.

"You are so selfish, Helen," said mummy, suddenly adopting a new line of attack. "You never think of anybody but yourself. And you are so unaffectionate. Why are you so unaffectionate? Come back in here while I'm shouting at you."

Years before she had shaken Daisy for wriggling when she was being smacked. I hastily swallowed the bubble of hysterical laughter welling inside. To laugh in her face was folly. Laura had proved it time and again. Laura claimed she never meant to laugh when we were comparing welt marks after a thrashing. She once had a welt that showed all the fingers of mummy's hand. She had been immensely proud of it and was very disappointed that it had faded the next day as she had hoped to show everyone at school.

Mummy wouldn't speak to any of us all day. Usually she would relent and ask, "Did that tonguing I gave you do you any good?" but not today. She was enjoying her moment of high passion too much.

"What are you crying for now?" Sarah accused me somewhat spitefully, because she had also been lashed with the forked tongue.

"I never said a word," I protested.

Damn Huge anyway. What sort of a useless man was he? He had flown to North Africa on 12 December and wasn't coming back until New Year's Eve. Two-and-a-half weeks of sun while I endured two-and-a-half weeks of domestic hell.

It wasn't healthy to be happy all the time.

No one mentioned sheep at dinner. No one dared say very much. You could have cut the atmosphere with a knife. Daddy remained hangdoggish. Daisy resumed her belligerent bravado. Sarah, trying to do something fancy with the mince, had burnt it to the bottom of the saucepan.

"Let's run away," Daisy suggested as we washed up. Even Henry wouldn't eat the mince mistake.

"Where are we going to run to? Nobody wants us."

Daisy sighed. "I don't care, Helen. The two rams fought on the way to Swatragh and had blood dripping from their skulls when we got there. I had to spray all the sheep with red spray on their heads so no one could see it was blood. Daddy dithered the entire day. He can't function when mummy isn't speaking to him."

"Did they sell well?" Daisy had more cop-on than many gave her credit for.

"Yes, really well; so when the auctioneer's cheque comes we will have plenty of money to run away with. We will just have to get to the cheque before mummy does."

"We could go to Jennifer in Kinelvin," I suggested.

"Yes," said Daisy, "Kinelvin can't be any worse than Derryrose."

"Famous last words," I smiled.

On Christmas morning we thought the end had come. The end of the Morris, and of life as we knew it. Sarah and Laura and the twins had gone to the carol service in Sarah's brown Metro, leaving Daisy and me to mummy and daddy and the Morris.

The car choked bravely to life after the second attempt down the drive. Daisy and I who had been pushing leapt into the back seat. The car coughed and stopped.

"Damn and blast," said mummy choosing to forget that it was Christmas and Sunday. "This is your fault, Kenneth. You let those ungrateful daughters of yours drive the devil out of our car. They are doing handbrake turns and speeding."

Daddy said nothing. He was treading a knife-edge, temporarily back in favour since presenting her with perfume and chocolates that morning, but it wouldn't take much to knock him back into dogdom. Daisy told me that he had sent her into the shop to choose the presents which had cost as much as the hornie ram.

"But he was willing to spend any amount to pacify her. He dare not tell her that eight of the eleven lambs did belong to me. And one thing about daddy, he's not cute."

"Oh dear," said daddy. "I see what the problem is now. We aren't going anywhere this morning."

"Why not?" we chorused.

"Why can't you fix it?" demanded mummy.

"Because the car has run out of petrol," said daddy.

"There is gooseberry wine in the house," I suggested, because I had seen the funny side. "Will we try that?"

"Don't be so stupid, Helen," mummy snapped. She had abandoned her sense of humour on the green grassy slopes of the Boyne.

Daisy and I nudged each other. The nudge meant "Deliberation over, we are definitely running away."

CHAPTER SIXTEEN

S o on the second of January we ran away. Daisy
had intercepted the auctioneer's cheque from
the postman on the Thursday. We were ready.

But there were numerous practicalities connected
with escape from Derryrose. Of primary consideration
was how to get into Magherafelt to catch the Dublin
bus. Stealing Sarah's Mini Metro was the obvious
theoretical answer but only an innocent, unfamiliar
with Derryrose politics, would have considered this a
serious option. On New Year's Day the Morris had
been dispatched to Moneymore to collect Granny
McBride for the dinner party given annually in her
honour.

It never got there. Two miles from home daddy
changed down to overtake a tractor. There was a
sickening grinding noise and the gearbox fell out on
to the road.

Within hours Sarah had her Metro car keys
strapped to her chastity belt and a tariff of 10p a mile
imposed on all passengers. She stood to make her
first million by the end of the Christmas holidays
because the Morris had been hospitalised as a terminal
case. Daddy through a sense of misguided loyalties

persisted in employing Cecil Simpson, Willie the Half-wit's father, as mechanic. Cecil had been with him the day he bought the car. We didn't expect to see our car for a long, long time.

"We will have to let Sarah in on our plan," Daisy said eventually. It was Monday night, after Granny McBride's dinner, and Sarah was driving her back to Moneymore. Daisy and I were finishing the Christmas port in my bedroom. Daisy had perked up considerably since the Johnboy incident, and the impending excitement had lifted most of my depression fog.

"She can be bribed to hold her tongue. We'll pay her 20p a mile."

"No," said Sarah, "It's the stupidest, most adolescent idea you have had yet. I won't help you run away unless you leave a note for mummy. Think how worried she will be. Think of what the rest of us will have to listen to."

I wanted suddenly to pull her smooth fair hair out by the handful. I could have pleaded temporary insanity.

"Don't be such a self-righteous prig," said Daisy crossly. "You can tell her that we have gone. We will give you 20p a mile each to take us into Magherafelt."

"£5," said Sarah, "to ease my conscience."

I really thought that we weren't going to make it the next morning. The bus for Dublin passed daily through Magherafelt at 11.18 a.m. At 11.05 we were in the car and ready to go. Sarah got back out again because she said she couldn't go into Magherafelt in her old Stranmillis sweatshirt.

Daisy, manic and desperate to be away, roared, "Get into this bloody car, Sarah, before I pull your ponytail out."

On the outskirts of the town she braked down to 30mph to obey the speed laws. Then she got stuck behind a bread van and refused to overtake on a straight bit of road because it was a built-up area. It crossed my mind that in her own convoluted way, perhaps, she wanted to discourage us from running away, but whether it was for charitable or selfish reasons I had no idea.

The Dublin express was pulling out when we turned the corner into Broad Street. Daisy muttered a dangerous oath, leapt from the Metro and chased after the bus. Fascinated I watched her batter on the door yelling, "Stop! Stop! Open up. Open up."

"Oh, God," I heard Sarah plead to the Almighty.

Daisy threw my handbag on to the bus and yelled manically, "Now you will have to wait."

We didn't give Sarah a backward glance. Her part in our escape was completed. She had been paid £5 to return to Derryrose and face the music.

The bus driver was a rude cheeky man. He snapped the money for our fare out of Daisy's hand.

"There are seats at the back of the bus," he told us. In fact the bus was empty but for a nun at the front, eating solidly through a box of Quality Street.

"You'd think that nun would practise a bit of

charity and offer us a sweet," Daisy whispered to me.

"No," I whispered back. "Charity means love not generosity."

It was exciting being a runaway. In Armagh we had tea in a cake shop. Runaways in novels always ate fish and chips but we were saving that treat for Beshoffs in Dublin.

There was no answer from Kinelvin when we phoned before the fish and chips, no answer after the fish and chips and no answer before and after a glass of Guinness at the train station.

"Do you think she's not in or is she just not answering?" Daisy asked. The nun who had been devouring the chocolate on the Dublin bus was sitting just opposite us in the pub, drinking a pint of Guinness and reading a Jackie Collins novel. Bit racy for a nun I thought.

"She is probably still so hungover from New Year's Eve that she can't lift the phone," I comforted. "Let's keep going."

"Howarya?" said the nun suddenly. "Are you going to Kerry too?"

We looked at her suspiciously. I had been at UCD with girls who had survived convent school but they had terrorised me with stories of sadistic Brides of Christ whipping them for displaying body language. I had never heard a story about a normal nun yet.

"Yes, we are," said Daisy bravely. The nun didn't look that old actually. To be fair, not any older than us. It was her habit and our attitudes that aged her.

"Great," said the nun. "So am I. Will you have another Guinness?"

The nun was called Dolores and after five minutes of Irish conversation we discovered that her brother had done Ag at UCD and her cousin was none other than Mighty Mick of the Shovel-like Hands who had shifted Laura in a cupboard the second week we had been in Dublin. Dolores was very impressed that Laura and Mick had shifted steadily for over two years.

"It is as well," I commented when Daisy had gone to get another drink, "that you did not take a vow of temperance."

Dolores sucked into a cigarette. I was not familiar with Catholic nun etiquette. I did not know whether to call her Sister Dolores or not.

"Hum," said Dolores, "I have been paralysed all week. I was visiting my granny in Portstewart. The bloody woman carries Ireland's morals on her back. She prayed for me when she caught me smoking in the toilet. I couldn't get the butt to flush away. It kept floating to the top. At least at home there is a decent drinks cabinet and the brother from Ag to blame it on. Granny is that proud I am a nun she gave me a box of Quality Street leaving."

She scrabbled around in the yellow rucksack at her feet and produced the box.

"Help yourself. If you don't the brother will, and he's fat enough as it is."

I said I had never seen a fat Kerryman yet. I was fascinated by the way she could balance her fag with her lips and talk at the same time.

She said she had never known Presbyterians who drank.

We told her about running away. She had never heard of Kinelvin. But she said we could stay with her if we wanted. "Aren't you friends of my cousin Mick?"

The train to Tralee went round the world for a shortcut. "Maybe," I suggested, with more hope than conviction, "maybe she will be waiting for us at the train station."

She wasn't.

"We hate to impose on you." I was mortified. Running away wasn't much crack after all. We didn't know whether to turn right or left at the train station to go to Kinelvin.

The Bride of Christ was delighted.

I didn't recognise Ollie Murphy but he seemed to know me on sight. He blushed actually, and a nasty suspicion jumped into my head. Had I shifted him some dark night?

"Helen Gordon," said Ollie, "this is a great honour. You must sleep in my bed tonight."

I felt a little flattered of course but more baffled than flattered. I couldn't possibly have shifted him. I would have remembered. He explained himself.

"I was in 4th Ag when you were in second year. The half of my class were in love with you in your tiny miniskirts. There wasn't another girl like you in the Ag block. I would have tried to shift you myself if it hadn't been for your boyfriend."

Well, that was something. At least I hadn't shifted him. But I never had a boyfriend in 2nd Ag.

"Which boyfriend?"

He laughed loudly to intimate that this was what he expected me to say. "Which boyfriend? The English one. Didn't you shift him on and off?"

Richard.

"No," I said firmly. "Never. We were just friends. On and off."

"You don't say?" Ollie sighed at his lost opportunity. "If only I had known that. Are you sure you remember the one I mean? Curly hair. Awfully grand. We were all convinced you were married."

"It was an open marriage," I smiled.

Dolores's father knew the Montgomerys. "Are you quite sure you want to go there?"

"Quite sure," we said. "Our sister is married to Charlie Montgomery. She had a baby at the start of November."

"Stay here tonight," Mr Murphy proposed, "and maybe you will have changed your mind by tomorrow morning. If not I will drive you out to Kinelvin. There is no bus service."

Next morning Dolores cooked us a huge breakfast. "I'm due back at the convent today," she explained, "or I would go with you for the spin."

Ollie Murphy had slept on the sitting-room sofa, just so he could tell how he had had me in his bed. I woke him up before we left to thank him.

"Will you give me a little kiss?" I asked him. He didn't deserve it of course. Flattered and all as I had been I had spent a rotten night in his bed. Maybe running away had shattered my nerves. Maybe it was the memory of something else.

Ollie was delighted to kiss me. And in the end I was delighted that he had. I had slipped up badly not shifting him at UCD.

CHAPTER SEVENTEEN

Kinelvin was quite a distance from Tralee and
the warm hospitality of the Murphy family.
Daisy and I exchanged a couple of embarrassed glances
before I said, "Oh Mr Murphy, this is quite a distance,"
in my most humble voice. And there still had been
no answer from Kinelvin when we had telephoned
earlier.

"Nearly there," said Mr Murphy, and braked and
stopped the car on the edge of the road.

"This is Kinelvin," he announced. "I don't like
leaving you on the edge of the road but only a
Montgomery would attempt the lane to the house in
weather like this."

It was raining again, a soft month in Kerry. Poor
Mr Murphy said he felt unchristian leaving us—
abandoning us he phrased it.

"But I will be back this way in an hour," he said
as much to himself as to us. "If you change your
minds I'll take you back to Tralee with me."

We hadn't walked ten yards up the rutted lane
before the reason for Mr Murphy's hesitancy became
apparent. The tree-canopied grandeur we had entered
from the road ended abruptly and we exited into a

field. Along an overgrown hedge along the edge of the field two soggy ribbons of wheel-tracks discouraged further progress.

"Maybe he got the wrong lane," said Daisy pointing to a donkey a field away watching with what I classed a critical expression. "That donkey looks like he is laughing at us," she added.

"Yes," I agreed feeling the first slow weep of damp through my boots. "And where has the avenue disappeared to?"

So we continued along the wheel-tracks up the edge of the field, but only because there was nothing else we could do and nowhere else we could go. Once my boots had filled with water I was past caring if we ever found the house.

"Well now," said Daisy, "How peculiar."

Having struggled the length of the field we rejoined the canopy of the rutted avenue and caught first glimpse of Kinelvin.

"Oh God," I said, "What a hole." It was even worse than Derryrose.

Our troubles were only beginning. Years ago Laura had persuaded mummy to allow us to sit up and watch *The Hound of the Baskervilles* on late-night television. Laura, High Priestess of the Cheap Thrill. She had me petrified before it ever started, spinning me her interpretation of the story which was that the hound was really Jack the Ripper. I had been taken to bed at the first commercial break, a shattered wreck, and had spent the night lying rigid between mummy and daddy waiting for the terrible baying of the terrible hound.

Well the hound had found me at last. I could hear him coming for me. From the look on Daisy's face she could hear it as well.

"Jesus Christ," said Daisy, "It's coming for us." The noise was everywhere in the wooded lane, pounding in my head like a hangover. We hadn't time to drop all and run. Like two myxomatosis rabbits caught in the glare of car headlights we waited for the noise to get us.

But it wasn't the Bloodhound from Hell of course. It was a pack of excited fox hounds and I almost fainted with relief when a river of them surrounded me. Now I could see them and touch them and shout at them to get down off me the noise didn't sound so hellish any more. I laughed a bit and enjoyed them and my own foolishness.

But Daisy grasped me, a vice grip that clamped my arm through the layers of wax coat and woolly jumper.

"Calm down, Daisy," I laughed without looking up. "It's only foxes they savage."

She didn't reply. Nor did she release my arm which had begun to ache with the pressure of her fingers around it.

"No, no, no," she repeated.

I looked up.

The shock was completely physical. The way you feel just before you throw up. Searing heat, cold sweat, blind panic. I felt the colour drain from my face.

In front of me, my shock mirrored on his face, stood Richard Knight.

No, no, no.

"Well girls," said a squat stocky Kerryman (the huntsman, I thought vaguely). "Have you lost yourselves?" He must have thought we were tourists.

Daisy gabbled inarticulately. I couldn't understand what she said. I stood rooted by my water-filled boots and the eyes of Richard in front of me.

"It's all right, Barry," I heard Richard say. "I know these ladies," and then there was a lot of noise and suddenly we were surrounded by Montgomeries yahooing and tally-hoing and making surprised noises. I saw Charlie slide from his horse and heard myself make a gentle joke about him feeding us to the hounds.

I saw myself greet his brother George, his father and his grandfather. I felt myself smile at George whom I found rather attractive.

And all the time my heart and my head pounded with Richard.

"Won't Jennifer be surprised to see you?" George was carrying my rucksack and I was leading his horse. Somewhere else, behind us, Charlie was leading Daisy. The others, Richard, were away with the hounds.

"Didn't she get our letter?"

"Postman never comes near us."

"We tried to telephone," I said, "We tried your number a dozen times yesterday. There was no answer."

"The phone hasn't worked for a week. And the

telephone man can't get his van up the lane in this weather."

"We have run away," I announced as we reached the house.

"From our mother," Daisy added.

"But your mother is a lovely woman," George said. I was aware I was smiling coyly at him. How could I?

"Jennifer, Jennifer." George shouted, "Yo, Jennifer. It was her turn to stay with Freddie today," he explained, "She will be round the back in the kitchen."

"Cooking?" I asked, incredulous.

"Hey, Charlie," said George, "Helen wants to know if Jennifer is in the kitchen cooking for us."

Charlie handed George his horse and said, "Don't be silly Helen. I didn't marry my wife to have her cook for us. Come along round the back. There is a lock on the front door."

I had time to wonder as we walked round the side of the house who was the alarm protecting, those in the house or those wishing to enter.

"Surprise, Jennifer," Charlie shouted, opening the back door into a hall littered with wellies and coats and sundry unmentionable horrors.

The kitchen was full of dogs and steam and though we often criticised the housekeeping at Derryrose, at least dishes were washed sometimes. I saw the pile of dirty dishes before I saw my sister. She was frantically twiddling at the knob of an ancient wireless set and through the crackles I heard the unmistakable *Archers* theme music.

"Oh shit," she said, "I've missed it. This weather is making reception impossible."

Then she saw Daisy and me. "Hello there," she said. "What are you doing here?"

We told her we had run away while she made us a cup of tea, and Charlie, with considerable skill, changed the baby's nappy at the far end of the table. It was fascinating.

"This," said Jennifer, "is where I gave birth to that rat. Now that he is dry take the opportunity to coo over him. He is much better-looking than his cousins."

Freddie Montgomery looked much the same as any other baby. Familiar with the procedure I tickled his belly and examined his fingers and toes.

"Have you developed any maternal instincts?" I asked when I had become bored with displaying an interest.

"Not a bit," she told me cheerfully. "I find him mind-blowingly boring. He sleeps, he cries, he feeds. But Charlie has sprouted into an amazing nurse. He actually enjoys bathing it and changing it though he had to pretend that he does it out of duty, or the others would call him a pansy."

She made a face in the direction of her husband who with Daisy was patting the baby's head and talking child husbandry.

Jennifer lit a cigarette and patted the terrier she was nursing. "Richard Knight is here for a few days," she said casually.

"I know," I said evenly. "I've seen him already.

George carried my bag. He's a real screw isn't he?"

That night I couldn't sleep in my high musty double bed. Beside me, comfortable in her high double bed, Daisy made quiet night noises. Around me the air was velvet-black, heavy tapestry curtains blotting out the moonlight. Maybe there was no moonlight in Kerry. My bed was probably full of fleas. Tomorrow morning I would be wearing a waistband of chewed skin. Jennifer had only remembered that we required beds as we had made to retire.

"Oh God," she had said scratching her head, obviously loth to leave the fire which was scorching my front while a draught ripped at my back. "I forgot about beds." We followed her from the room like obedient children.

"Richard is in the spare room," she said, "But there is another bedroom in the attics. I'd better put the kettle on. You'll need hot-water bottles if you are under the roof."

The room under the roof had no electricity but Jennifer found candles with relative ease. "We don't have electricity half the time," she explained. "The wiring in this house is unfit for human consumption."

The room under the roof was romantic by candle-light. Predominantly displayed were two outsized double beds. Jennifer grinned obviously delighted with herself. "I knew there were beds in here. What more could you ask for? A double bed each. If they hadn't been here you would have had to share with

Richard and George."

Lying now in the one beside the window, furthest from the door, I decided I had to go to the loo. If only I could remember where it was. And if only I could make my way to it through the terrible blackness surrounding me to the light switch at the end of the hall. I might as well climb Everest. So I lay a bit longer and tried to think beautiful thoughts. But that was no use because I had no beautiful thoughts in my head, just a bursting desire to get to the loo.

Resigned, I rolled from the swaddling in the big bed. Not even baby Jesus in his manger in Bethlehem was as well wrapped up as me. The floorboards felt dusty and strange beneath my feet. I almost wanted to laugh it was so ridiculous.

It took a lifetime to circumnavigate Daisy's bed, but once into the hall I felt I was almost there. Just straight to the end and locate the light switch. Fumbling and groping and knowing the blackness of blindness. Such a relief to walk into the urn of pampas grass at the far end. The urn rattled alarmingly in the dark. And every floorboard protested loudly when I tramped on it.

Groped and groped and finally found the light switch.

Light flooding the hall, shocking me. As if I had smashed glass in the silence.

But the minute I could see I remembered the direction of the bathroom.

After the loo I decided not to go back to bed

immediately. I was confident of finding my way to the kitchen to warm a saucepan of milk. And warm milk especially laced with brandy is a marvellous sedative. The idea cheered me up so much I was even able to chuckle remembering the poster Daisy had pointed to as we left Magherafelt yesterday morning. "Booze Is the Devil's Vomit." The writer was obviously not an insomniac.

Assisting my descent to the bowels of the house was a shaft of Kerry moonlight, tracing patterns on the avenue trees.

"There is no mystery about the avenue," Charlie's father had told us at dinner. "My great-grandfather built the house for his English fiancée. He was organising the avenue when the flighty thing sent her governess to Ireland to tell him she was calling the whole thing off. She didn't want to leave Surrey she said. Old Fred was heartbroken and refused to finish the avenue."

Charlie's father's father laughed cynically at the story. "He hadn't the funds to finish it," he said. "And he wasn't so heartbroken over the filly that he couldn't marry the governess instead."

Once my milk had heated sufficiently I tripped along the dark halls of the bottom of the house in search of the brandy and the room with the fire. Surely the fire would still have some life in it? I had left my novel there earlier. I could drink the milk and have a read before going back to bed. Far better than ever being asleep.

Someone else had the same idea as me. Reflected in the firelight a thin curly-haired man was reading, a glass of sipping whiskey at his elbow. He looked up as I opened the door and came into the room. Courteously he stood up and set down his book.

"Helen," he said.

"Richard," I said back again.

CHAPTER EIGHTEEN

"But Helen, you must be freezing." He advanced towards me arms outstretched to draw me towards the fire. Instinctively the gentleman regardless of his opinion of the lady. "I came to get a shot of brandy for my milk," I explained. At least with Richard there was no necessity to apologise or excuse my drinking. I hold that to his eternal credit. "You can't sleep?" he enquired, pouring me a generous shot from an old bottle. When we were friends at UCD he had always said he could tell how well I had slept by the magnitude of my pout the next morning. "It's a terrible bed." I felt quite calm once I had knocked back the brandy and milk. Not traumatised at all. "Another?" he asked politely. "Thank you, no." Maybe the sick awfulness of seeing him earlier had been a figment of my rampant imagination.

Out of the companionable silence Richard said, "I'm surprised by your choice of *The Bostonians*, Helen. I can't ever imagine you with aggressive feminist tendencies or an affection for Henry James."

A nice calm conversation about a subject that was neutral territory. "Oh it belongs to Sarah," I said. "She is the one with feminist sympathies. She gave it to me because she was disgusted with the ending. Weak, she described it."

He handed me my book, so I flicked through the pages to find my place while he lifted what I assumed was his own novel. It had Somerville and Ross: *French Leave* on the spine. "Richard," mischievously, "I can't ever imagine you with feminist tendencies."

He caught my eye and laughed. Richard didn't laugh very often which was a pity. He had a nice laugh. "I wondered how long it would take you, Helen. You still haven't lost your touch."

"That book," I was severe. "It might be a Somerville and Ross but it reeks of feminist tendencies."

"Yes but it has a weak ending too."

Richard and I both belonged to that category of reader who reads the first chapter followed by the final chapter, followed by the rest of the book.

"Can't you sleep?" I asked suddenly, having waded through a tedious bit of Victorian description.

"It's a terrible bed." We smiled again at each other.

"You know, Richard," I said setting *The Bostonians* down. "I think someone died in my bed. There is a lace curtain on top of the blankets. Makes me think of a shroud."

"Don't panic," he smiled. "I found a piece of carpet being used as a blanket on my bed. I think I know where the lace belongs. Solves a mystery actually. Since I came here I have been convinced that the table-cloth in the dining-room is really a bedspread. Shall we investigate it more closely in the morning?

And swap them to see if anyone notices?"

"Well," I grinned, "Jennifer certainly won't. She has never made a bed in her life. And if tonight's dinner was anything to go by, she still can't cook."

"You caught her on a bad day. We have had carrots in the stew every other day this week."

I believe dinner had started life as mince and onion but the gravy had gelled into bloodclots and the potatoes were hard and cold, as if they had been boiled the week before and stored in the fridge. They may well have been. No one commented on these culinary shortcomings. Their passage to the stomach had been eased by an excellent red wine George had dug up in our honour. "For our guests," he had explained. Poor George was the only family member who was aware of the deficiencies in Kinelvin's housekeeping. Earlier, while Jennifer, Daisy and I drank tea, ate biscuits and talked women's talk, Charlie had washed the dishes and George had swept the kitchen floor and the hall, and had paired the wellies neatly at the back door.

"Shall we offer to help?" Daisy had asked timidly.

"Certainly not," said Jennifer appalled. "They are showing off because you are here. The floor doesn't need brushing. George mopped it yesterday. It is still clean."

"Do you ever do housework?"

"Oh, not if I can help it," she replied airily. "Though I sometimes do cook the dinner at night. George and Charlie are well trained. They forbid that

I should slave. I am the Mistress of Kinelvin."

Charlie had been eavesdropping as he cleared away the cups. "If we wanted a housekeeper we would have kept your mother on full time," he said, winking mysteriously at Jennifer.

"Mummy was desperate when she was here," Jennifer explained. "She wouldn't let us touch Freddie unless we were sterilised with boiling water first. And she slapped me when she caught me smoking and breast-feeding at the same time. Hardly any wonder I didn't develop a maternal instinct. She even nagged because everybody in the house was wearing odd socks. Only she noticed. Charlie says if I ever show signs of turning into my mother he will run away."

"You know, Richard," I added, "You have to feel sorry for our mother. No sooner does she get rid of Jennifer, her delinquent daughter, than big trouble descends from Donegal."

I told him how Aunt Maisie had set fire to herself and her fortune and had demanded sanctuary from us. Richard was delighted. Aunt Maisie was one of his favourite characters in the Gordon soap opera. Aunt Maisie and my mother. Richard had a weakness for psychotic women. "Is your old aunt still raping and pillaging?"

"Of course. She was very good, suspiciously good in fact for the first week but that was only because she thought we were going to have her committed."

"To an asylum?"

"Not quite. To an old people's home with Granny

McBride. But she is too cheeky. At least Granny McBride does what she is told even if she is a murderer." Richard knew about Granny McBride. "Then," I said, "she continued being precocious and impossible. She caught daddy streaking mummy's hair. Pulling the hair through the holey cap with a crochet needle. Laura and mummy bought a kit between them but Laura's highlights were a disaster. Her hair is too red. It's like carrots and parsnips now. She hid in the house for days afterwards. Aunt Maisie says, "Jennifer, you shouldn't encourage Kenneth to be a hairdresser. It's so poofy.'"

"Brilliant," said Richard. "Did your mother stab her?"

"Not yet. So Aunt Maisie says, 'What colour is your hair really, Jennifer? The natural shade I mean. It has been an artificial colour for so long now.' So mummy took her frustrations out on us instead. When her hair was finished she couldn't find her favourite curling brush, so we had to search the house for it. And none of the six brushes we found was her favourite. So she slapped Sarah because she said Sarah was bound to be the culprit; she is always fussing with her hair. Then she slapped Laura because she said that whenever the hair-drier goes missing it is always Laura who has it. And all the time Aunt Maisie is watching her, smirking. She probably hid the curling brush for badness. And mummy getting madder by the second because her new hair is drying and she hasn't got the brush she wants to style it."

"What did she do?"

"Leapt into the car, drove off with a screech of wheels to Ruth Paisley's house. Ruth is good with hair."

"And Aunt Maisie?"

"Once she had driven mummy away she decided to touch up her own hair. It has been dyed black since she was forty. Mummy came home penitent with a can of draught Guinness each for us and found Aunt Maisie had dyed daddy's hair black too. Daddy thought he looked magnificent. Needless to say she drank all the Guinness herself. Daisy and I felt really left out so we bought a bottle of red dye and did our hair too."

"I noticed," said Richard.

"The dye only stays in for half a dozen washes," I explained, "but we liked the effect so much that we have been doing it every couple of weeks since."

I stopped talking suddenly. This was how Richard and I used to be. Helen the foolish and Richard the long-suffering. Even then we had a list of permitted subjects. My family was on the list. My feelings were not.

I stood up. "I think I will retire," I told him, "or I will be good for nothing tomorrow. Jennifer has promised Daisy and me a couple of real ditches. I haven't ridden for so long I will probably land on my head in the first one and drown unromantically."

He stood up and we stood smiling at each other for a minute. I wanted to touch him, just his jumper, but I didn't. He wouldn't have understood. "Goodnight, Richard," I said instead.

Next morning Jennifer took Daisy and me out. For some mad reason I had expected Kinelvin tack to shine and the Kinelvin stable yard to smile brightly with paint.

I must read the wrong books.

But the horses were animals. "I remember you as being timid, Daisy," Jennifer had said over breakfast. "You better have Grandpa's mare. Even mummy rode her in a skirt when she was here."

"What about me?" I asked. "I'm timid too."

"Rubbish." She smiled wickedly. "You are too modest, Helen. You ride nearly as well as me."

"But I always fall off," I protested.

"Only because you are so busy looking round you. Take Lucy. She's a real goer."

So we scrambled on. Lucy the real goer seemed well-behaved. George had ridden her only yesterday. She was well-exercised. I had nothing to worry about. Richard would not have to pull me out of a ditch after all.

Jennifer, in front, pulled her red hunter left and cantered through the trees lining the avenue. Innocently Lucy and I followed, Daisy and Grandpa's rocking-horse behind us. Jennifer popped over what looked like a bit of long grass and with my mind only half on the job I followed her.

I was not prepared for the four-foot drop on the

other side, and Lucy was not prepared for the thump I made on her back when I banged back down into the saddle. So she executed a couple of nimble bucks, giving me just enough time to bellow an undignified oath as I slipped off her and on to my head in the mud. There was some convincing teeth-rattling on contact with the ground.

Lucy, delighted to be freed of her skill-less rider, gave another couple of joyful bucks and raced up the field, Jennifer and the red hunter in hot pursuit.

Behind me, on the other side of the fence, Daisy had reined in the rocking-horse and was watching, amused. "I wish I could bottle the look on your face," she said.

CHAPTER NINETEEN

"So then she went whizzing arse over tit and landed in a pile in a puddle."

Jennifer and Daisy were getting great mileage out of my fall through lunch. I was smiling bravely, just thankful I hadn't knocked any teeth out.

"Her face was a picture," said Daisy.

"And when I got back with Lucy she was on her feet blowing like a bull," said Jennifer. "Bloody leathers are too long" she yells and shortens them in about four seconds. And leaps back into the saddle. It was priceless. In the yard before we left she needed a block to get up."

Daisy giggled. Uncharitably I remembered that she had made Jennifer jump Grandpa's rocking-horse down the bank for her. Daisy had no desire to repeat my acrobatics.

"And Helen took the rest of the banks as if she was at Punchestown."

"Not quite." I might as well confess. "I couldn't hold Lucy. She pulled the arms out of me. Bit of a difference between a stabled hunter and a grass-fat pony."

"Never mind," said Charlie's father. "In a couple

of days you will be falling off as often as the rest of us. We have a competition: 'Who Can Fall Off The Most In One Season.' George is leading at the moment but maybe you will win if you keep this up."

"You will have to fall off at least once a day to beat me," said George proudly.

"I came off twice yesterday," said Richard. "Jennifer's hunter is cross-eyed, I swear."

"And she twists when she bucks," said Jennifer.

They were all so cheerful and dirty and easily pleased. I played with my bowl of home-made soup and listened to the conversation bouncing round me. Charlie had made the soup and it was dreadful. Once I looked up and found Richard's eyes on me. He winked.

"So," said Jennifer, "what is planned for this afternoon?"

"Well," said Daisy quickly, "I thought I might try out the piano in the drawing-room. If that's all right."

"Certainly, my dear," said Charlie's father. "My wife used to play all the time before she ran away. Her music will still be there if the rats haven't eaten it."

Richard said, "I'll take Helen into Tralee to phone her mother."

"How far do you live from here?" I asked him when we had safely negotiated the avenue and were out on the road to Tralee, just Richard and me in the comfortable filth of the Kinelvin pick-up with a car-crazy terrier on my knee.

"Quite a bit."

Maybe he was afraid that if he gave directions I would take a notion and arrive on his doorstep next.

I got through to Derryrose immediately. Heart pounding, nervously I watched two 50p's slip down the throat of the phone and heard mummy's cautious "Hello?" Mummy is always cautious when she answers the phone in the middle of the day because she says that it is always someone wanting something, usually money.

"Mummy?" From the corner of my eye I could see Richard in the pick-up watching me. I waved to him to give myself confidence.

"Helen? I hate your father today. He has lost the signet ring I bought him when we got engaged. There were two lambs born last night and he was more excited than when any of you children arrived. He was dancing in the kitchen until I asked him where the ring was. He thinks he left it in the byre. He's out there searching for it again. This really is the last straw."

"Yes, mummy."

"And the bloody Morris is still in the garage. That half-wit Cecil Simpson hasn't even looked at it yet. I went to sort him out this morning and Slack Alice told me that he was fixing somebody else's car last night and it went up in flames. He dropped the end of his cigarette into the carburettor. Good riddance."

"Is he dead?"

"Of course not. Slack Alice said that his stubble saved him. But he is in hospital with multiple burns.

And the Morris will be there for at least another month."

"What are you driving?"

"Simpsons gave us a car. Willie's. A Mark 2 Escort that he rallies in. The horn plays 'Clementine' and he has a thousand furry toys in the back window."

"Willie's gold car?"

"Yes with four spotlights on the front. Your father thinks it's the greatest car he has ever driven. Your father..."

Gently I set the phone down and trotted out to Richard in the pick-up. He was ready with a handful of change.

"Richard we have got a new car. Gold Mark 2 Escort. Can you give me a loan?"

"Those metallic cars were very trendy in their day," he grinned at me.

Mummy unaware of my temporary desertion was still ranting when I picked the phone up again. It was Sarah's turn.

"I can't understand why she is so selfish. She must take after her father. She won't share her Metro with me. She says I'm a reckless driver. I hate the Escort. It cramps my style. And every Fenian in Magherafelt waves at me when I drive past. Uncle Reggie says Mark 2 Escorts are IRA staff cars."

"Mummy, my money is finished."

"What?"

"My money is finished."

"Helen, Helen, where are you?"

I was cut off.

"How is your mother?" Richard asked politely when I rejoined him in the pick-up.

"Very well thank you," I replied laughing.

The Gordons were all, or nearly all, going to the church social. I was not dressed for the occasion. Hair was too untidy and I was wearing purple desert boots and black jeans. Had a bottle of Slimline tonic water in the pocket of my wax coat to mix with the gooseberry wine at home. Daisy and I stepped off the Dublin bus and into the off-licence.

My family were the only family to arrive without a massive offering of tinfoil-covered sandwiches. As a hungry teenager Laura used to eat the fillings out of the sandwiches and flush the bread down the loo. She said that she could get white bread any day of the week but never Mars Bar filling.

Once she brought an empty box to the social.

"Sandwiches," she had smiled and followed a helpful lady's directions as to where she should deposit them. Was it Mrs Mulholland the organist? She was wearing a blue furry hat tonight with a jaunty feather over the left ear. And ruby wool tights, the type mummy wears when she wants to be a rebel. Maybe mummy is a trendsetter to the Mrs Mulhollands of this world.

Laura deposited the empty box in the Ladies and read a novel throughout the speeches. Historical romance I think; *The Royal Road to Fotheringay* perhaps—mummy has a thing about the Tudor period. Laura crammed the box with buns afterwards. She had no adolescent hang-ups about being overweight.

Mummy had streaked her hair again. I'm sure it must be ready to fall out in handfuls. I didn't mention it at the door of the social because I wanted to wait for a less nice atmosphere. Presbyterians believe that beauty is skin-deep; virtue to the bone. She was pleased to see Daisy and me—good omen that.

D and I came straight home and missed the social. As always, beneath the shower is the hottest place in Derryrose. I have just drunk a glass of gooseberry wine and tonic water and am about to have a mug of Ovaltine—to hide the booze smell before the parents return.

Daddy was wearing the tie I bought him for Christmas. Dark red silk with navy blobs on it. Wonder where he has hidden the one Daisy got him. Trendy grey polyester with wild purple and yellow flowers traced on it. Too trendy for him, daddy thinks. I noticed Bobby Lennox wearing the one we got him for his birthday. He wiggles his hips when he walks. So does Aunt Maisie. I think this wine has mellowed me. I feel like laughing because the Ovaltine is disgusting. It is the last cup of Ovaltine I will ever drink. Oh well, life is made of learning experiences.

I remember a burst of creativity once when I made grated cheese and onion sandwiches for the social. Daddy was so impressed with them he kept the box in the car, brought them home and ate them himself.

I am hungry but of course the cupboard is bare. I dare not drink any more. Maybe I should drink gooseberry wine when I am writing. I float on regardless, uncluttered, unhesitating. "Oh yes Helen, our daughter, the alcoholic novelist. Spends her money as fast as she makes it—on gooseberry bushes."

Daisy and I had a couple of hours to kill in Dublin that afternoon before the bus left north. I bought five novels in a second-hand bookshop and Daisy got a flock-lined silk nighty in Dr Barnardos for £2.25. People will think we have money.

In Magherafelt, under cover of dark, with me standing guard Daisy stole a handful of pink flowers from a garden. She says they will look gorgeous pressed. My conscience smote me somewhat.

Mummy and daddy and Sarah returned from the social really excited. The gold Mark 2 Escort, Beauty, is now a permanent fixture in the Gordon household. What a priceless car.

Aunt May let it slip to mummy that Sandra Jackson proposed on St Valentine's Day, and it's not even a leap year. Ian gave her an £8.90 padded monstrosity of a valentine card. She brought it here to show Laura, and Sarah priced it in Magherafelt. Ian said yes. So they are engaged. Aunt May knows because Cousin Tracy, Sandra's only real friend, is to be bridesmaid. Tracy bought Sandra an egg-timer and a rolling-pin as engagement presents. She is to wear peach, the colour of lavatory paper. Ian and Co will wear navy tails and no hats.

Marvellous how there is someone for everyone in the world; even rejects can pair off together.

Daisy has been invited as Johnboy's woman. We are all going into Magherafelt tomorrow to buy her a chopping board.

CHAPTER TWENTY

I was sitting on the porch waiting for the sun to reappear from behind an obstinate cloud, drinking my latest cocktail—low-cal ginger ale, grapefruit juice, gooseberry wine—reading *Devoted Ladies*, an exceptionally brilliant Molly Keane novel. When the phone rang I expected it to be the Rabbit. Bloody Sandra never leaves our house these days. Sandra and the tasteful emerald. Her ring is not as large as the diamond Ian bought Sarah when they were engaged. Jennifer always claimed Sarah needed a sling on the arm that carried that crusher. Daisy was supposed to go to Belfast with Sandra to choose her knickers for her big day. Thank you, God, that I was not born Sandra Jackson.

Daisy, with convenient vagueness, headed off that morning on a flower hunt, her Wellworths plastic bag billowing in the breeze behind her. Daisy was the only woman in Ag who knew Harmony was an insecticide not a hairspray but she hides it well.

It was Huge on the telephone. Wanting to take me out for a drink. No questions, no explanations. No small talk to discover where I have been these past five months, no excuses to cover his desertion. I liked his style. We fixed a time.

Mummy gave me her navy cotton jumper, bought in a real shop, to wear on my date with Huge. I teamed it up with my new red, white and blue silk scarf bought from a newspaper offer. I tied my hair back and wore my new Oxfam canvas trousers which are extremely baggy. Mummy made me remove the purple desert boots, she said they spoiled the effect. Without them I looked like the heroine of a 1940s film.

Huge has changed his image. He must have realised he was not a New Man, nor ever likely to be one.

"I like simple motifs," he said of his olive Fruit of the Loom shirt. He winked as he said it. Sense of humour at last, perchance? I approved of the moleskin trousers and the brown brogues, but his short hair made him look like a football hooligan.

"Helen,"—Huge could never beat around the bush—"Helen, I want us to get back together again."

We had a mega shift on the kitchen floor of Derryrose. Spontaneous passion. And Huge was prepared to get his olive clothes dusty on the floor, was resigned to banging his head on the table leg, would risk my mother, the midnight prowler, walking in on us. Huge had improved tremendously.

We agreed to date again. But the dirty word, the big C, Commitment, was not to be mentioned between us. I insisted that we remain purely sexual.

Huge is back in favour. Before getting ready for bed I dug out my large photograph of him, that Daisy took at Bobby Lennox's Birthday Party. He looks like the sort of man he is. One who has remained friends with all his ex-women. He is reinstated in the frame that usually holds my UCD class photo with its illustrious undergraduate bravado. How simple life was then. Huge in his sportscoat is a very sexual photograph. I can think of a hundred reasons why I don't want to go out with him.

Daisy had done something dreadful. She didn't come back from her flower hunt at lunchtime as promised. The Rabbit went to Belfast alone to choose her underwear.

Daisy came home without flowers and without her Webb's *Irish Flora* but she had a pony with her. Where Gypsy the pony came from remains a mystery. Tall and ugly, she certainly didn't gallop out of a fairytale. Flaxen-haired princesses and Knights in Shining Armour do not ride off into the sunset on a tinker's pony. I know these things; I am a romantic novelist.

But, the tinker's pony. There were gypsies camped on the Toomestone road. Had she stolen the pony, I wondered. Worse, had she bought it?

Fantastically I imagined she had been given it in return for a handful of wild flowers and a copy of Webb's.

Of course, nobody trusted the gypsies. Every councillor in the country was petitioning to get rid of them. They were accused of many provincial atrocities, hitherto blamed on Catholics, but they never stole any of our hens so we never bothered about them.

Daisy secretly confessed that she had swapped the pony for a heifer calf. She had not consulted daddy because she said that he never counted his stock and remained undecided as to whether he was a farmer or Lord Bellamy.

It seems he took a senile fit when we were in Kerry and had become a photographer. Reels of his efforts lay abandoned round the house, in drawers, behind ornaments, beneath cushions. Mummy wouldn't let him leave them into the chemist because she said we couldn't afford to have them developed. She was tight with every penny because she wanted a flashy processed-pine kitchen unit in her brown-and-white bungalow.

Daisy especially was fascinated to discover daddy's photographic aspirations. She was even tempted to have a film developed at her own expense but mummy assured her that his talent was distinctly second-rate. Sarah said the pictures were mostly of sunsets. Daddy sat in the picture window in the dining-room and shot at the sunset through the curtains. He had first attempted to master the piano (his New Year's resolution) but fortunately had concluded that his forte was not the musical. Photography was at least a quieter alternative.

We all took a spin on Gypsy in the flat meadow, mummy included. Bareback, slipping, insecure, yelping manically. Gypsy was happy to walk and trot at varying rates but showed no enthusiasm to break into a canter. Bouncing, teeth chattering, we agreed she was one hell of a trotter. Mummy was rather selfish about sharing out the rides but then mummy had romantic visions of herself as Lady Godiva. I only hoped I was dead, buried and forgotten about the day she realised them.

"Lovely temperament," she said, meaning that Gypsy hadn't bucked, bitten or trampled anyone.

"Sandra phoned twice," Laura announced when we went indoors after the appropriate horsy husbandry. Laura never rode because she had fallen off once and her jaw went black for a month.

"Damn Sandra," said Daisy, "and damn her knickers and damn her wedding. And damn it, girls, but we will have to buy her a present."

"Well, I'm not buying the Rabbit an expensive present," said Laura decisively. "I don't want to buy her anything."

We were in Magherafelt. Laura was very taken with some Czechoslovakian wine glasses which were reduced from £50 to £12. To Laura this was a godsent opportunity. I felt that practical presents were more appreciated and suggested that Daisy bought her Christmas decorations, Laura bathroom scales, and Sarah and I a battery torch. "No," said Sarah, who put on her martyr act that day. "People will talk about us if we buy her foreign rubbish." She wanted to buy a brass statue of two bodies tastefully draped round each other. She got her way.

"Will she give us sherry?" I asked mummy.

"Will she feed us?" Laura asked mummy.

"Will she ask us lots of questions?" Daisy asked in horror.

"Yes," said mummy. "It will be a perfection of social niceties. Eva has studied the subject intensely. And Helen, please refuse if she offers you sherry. And please don't eat all her biscuits, girls. You are such savages when you are out."

Mummy's best horror story from our illustrious and dreadful childhoods was the afternoon she took us *en masse* to visit Aunt May. The dainty Aunt May had set a plate of biscuits in front of us and retreated. Mummy swears she blinked and all the biscuits were gone. All except a sad little fig-roll which none of us liked.

Sandra was not her usual self when she opened the front door. Strangely I felt a mite miffed. The Rabbit had no business being distant with us. We were kind to her; she owed us everything.

"Mammy," said Sandra when we had been ceremoniously seated in the good room. "Mammy, I only put these jeans on yesterday. And they are dirty already."

Eva picked a piece of fluff off her sweater and looked tearful.

Sandra opened our present.

"Hum," she said. "hum, how original."

"Yes," said Eva, "that's very different. I haven't seen anything like that before."

Oh God! We all saw it at the same moment. The bodies entwined in brass were both male.

"Yes," I said. "Thanks, Mrs Jackson, but I will have that sherry after all."

How did one comfort a blushing bride? Sandra was sitting there fraught with sexual fear. Horrific and awesome in a girl of twenty-six. And as a spinster I was in no position to advise her in such a delicate subject. Not with her mother sitting there, all ears.

I could imagine Eva saying, "I think it's time we had a little chat, Sandra," on the morning of the wedding while Sandra, reeking of Anais Anais and toothpaste, was watching from her window for the limousine.

And Sandra, forgivably overwrought, would begin weeping and her brilliant blue eye-shadow would run in rivers down her peach-coloured cheeks.

Poor little Rabbit with her pink-rimmed eyes.

CHAPTER TWENTY-ONE

"**D**aisy," said daddy, "your dress simply will not do for the wedding. I am not happy with it."

Daddy was sulking. He and mummy had gone to a band parade in Ballyronan the night before. When two collectors asked him for a contribution he felt in his pocket and found ninepence. Mummy, dressed in pink like Barbara Cartland, had said loudly, "Well I'm moving off from this embarrassing situation," and had left him to it.

It was the day before Sandra Jackson's wedding. Daisy and I were in the Tower Centre, Ballymena, with mummy and daddy. I had spent £2 in the second-hand bookshop on *Cider With Rosie* and was deliberating, "Can I afford to spend £4.09 on Mozart's Horn Concertos?"

"What's wrong with my dress? There is nothing in here," said Daisy as we were unwillingly led into River Island. What Daisy meant was "There is nothing in here that I can afford." She was ready to trail back out again, happy to wear her faded flowered dress. After all, said Daisy, who was going to be looking at her?

Daddy chose Daisy a suit and sent her to fit it on.

He told me that mummy had once had a suit like it. She had worn it as her going-away outfit at her own wedding, she had worn it as a guest at Johnny Paisley's wedding, she had worn it at Laura's christening. Daisy looked very pretty in the suit which was cream linen with a *broderie anglaise* finish on the sleeves and skirt. But the skirt was too tight on her comfortable hips.

"I can't buy it; I can't breathe in this skirt," she said.

Daddy was completely out of place in River Island. But he had sprayed his hair before leaving Derryrose so he was a man to be reckoned with.

"Hi you," he hailed the Glamorous Blonde behind the counter. "I want a bigger skirt." GB said, "There is only one skirt left and it's on the model." GB considered this the end of the conversation. Daddy thought not. Belligerently he said, "Well dear, you have just lost yourself a sale."

They took the big skirt off the model. GB kept frowning at Daisy as if it was her fault that she had big hips. At least Daisy didn't wear orange foundation. The big skirt fitted her.

"Oh Daisy," said mummy encouragingly, "You look just like a model." She jammed a silly-looking black straw hat on Daisy's head. Half the shop was watching but all knew better than to interfere.

Daddy made her buy the entire thing. Suddenly £4.09 for the Horn Concertos was a petty decision.

"Now Daisy," said mummy, the morning of the

wedding, "remember you were reared to be a little princess."

Daisy was very green. "It is not excitement," she explained when I was pinning up her hair, "and unlike you it is not a manic phobia about getting married. It's women's problems."

"A flower," said mummy suddenly, "you have no flower."

So at 1.45 p.m. with the wedding fifteen minutes and three miles away Daisy was hacking her way through the wilderness garden in search of a flower. She reappeared with her new stockings laddered and a yellow rosebud. There was some kind of spotted disease on the rose leaves but that was a minor detail.

"Don't tell mummy about the stockings," I comforted, "and she will never notice. They are skin-tone colour anyway."

"But it's sacrilegious," she protested, "to go to church with laddered nylons."

Reasonably I said, "And it's positively pagan to go with bare legs. And there is not another pair of tights in the house that colour."

Beneath my Laura Ashley dress I was wearing a pair of powder-blue stockings of Aunt Maisie's. Mummy and I were going to watch the proceedings and had to be properly dressed.

At the church mummy and Daisy had a row about the silly black hat. Daisy wanted to wear it tipped back on her head *Little House on the Prairie* style; mummy kept pulling it so far forward Daisy was blinded.

"Look," I said. "The video is watching you." Mummy forgot about Daisy immediately and joined all the other blonde heads and brown legs trying to be filmed.

Sandra looked really beautiful. Daisy said she had studied a hundred brides in a hundred issues of *Hello!* magazine and had designed the dress herself. And Dr Hunt's mother had sewn it together. Twisted John Jackson, unused to the limelight, shook as she led him up the steps to the church door. Sandra tossed her veil and was the happiest girl in the world.

And Johnboy had got his hair cut. The difference a haircut can make. I almost fancied him myself.

Johnboy had eyes for no one but Daisy.

"I've got the tents," I heard him tell her as he ushered her into the church behind the bride. "Have you asked Helen yet?"

Asked me what? What tents? Most mysterious.

Daisy had a hot flush after the service.

"Why didn't you take some tablets?" I asked, watching mummy from the corner of my eye. Mad to get on film she was making a great show of congratulating the happy couple.

"I wanted to drink at the reception," said poor prostrated Daisy, "But Johnboy tells me that Ian and Sandra have asked that the bar stay shut."

Ian and Sandra had also decreed that the toasts be drunk in orange juice. Naturally there was to be no dance in the evening. Reverend Robinson was very proud of them.

As Daisy was convinced she wouldn't survive the car drive to the reception we sneaked away during the churchyard photographs and had a few stiff ones in Kate's Pub which was just down the road. Wantonly to walk into a pub in Magherafelt is an act of flagrant rebellion. When Laura was at school she used to run into Kate's with an anorak over her head so our minister wouldn't recognise her.

"There was high drama in the Jackson camp this morning," Daisy told me as we ordered. "No one knew what side to pin their flower on."

"At least," I said, "you have Tracy to talk to. If you want to talk to her."

"You can take your hat off now," said Johnboy as they got into Sandra's car. "No way," said Daisy, "I bought this silly hat and I intend wearing it."

Everyone else had taken their hats off after the service. Except for Eva, who had

(a) paid a fortune for hers;

(b) had it cemented on her head;

(c) had a bald spot she was trying to conceal.

Delete as appropriate.

I was cleaning the bath and feeling Sarah-like when Daisy got home.

"Cleaning?" she said. "But your name isn't Sarah." She was still hatted and mysteriously tipsy.

"Why are you half-pissed?" I was eating the piece of wedding cake she brought me home, having grown scared of sleeping with it beneath my pillow. I never dreamed of anybody.

"The waitress was Linda Patterson who used to bully you at primary school. Laura and you fought her once. Laura held her and you hit her."

"Linda of the childbearing hips?"

"Yes, she put gin in my Lucozade for me. Did mummy point you out Ian's parents?"

Ian's father had made his money from door furniture and fitted bathrooms. He wore navy spats at the wedding. Mrs Flemming wearing a huge white straw lampshade on her head had driven to the reception in a white convertible car with the lid down.

"The food was very posh," said Daisy. "Avocado. Then spinach-and-bacon soup. Mrs Flemming said she was sure it came out of a packet. I really enjoyed her. She sent back her sauté potatoes because they were swimming in oil and her Pavlova because it had only one strawberry on it."

"Were you at the top table?"

"No, her voice carries well."

To the tents. Johnboy and Daisy wanted Huge and me to accompany them on a camping weekend. We were going to sleep in tents, build a campfire and eat out of tins.

Huge was horribly enthusiastic about the camping idea. Huge had been a Boy Scout. When he was young and wild Huge had seduced his first woman on a blanket on the ground. Huge offered to take his new car. Johnboy, a Maxi driver, was overwhelmed. He bought numerous bags of crisps and admired the Merc at great length. Huge admired my sunburn but said my peppermint dungaree shorts were the worst he had ever seen.

After a stop at a vintage rally *en route* we camped in Rathmullan on the shore of Lough Swilly. Johnboy pitched his tent in minutes but ours was an inflatable igloo and it had a leak. It took hours to find glue and get the leak stuck and Johnboy and Huge refused to feed us famished females until it was finished. Male bonding and all that. Once they were done I lured Huge into the igloo for a fortifying shift before dinner.

Meanwhile a hatchback car with a flat wheel drove into our bit of campsite loaded with wood. The driver told us he was organising a beach party and invited us along.

So Daisy and Johnboy, ever enthusiastic, ever keen, gathered sticks for the campfire. Huge and I resumed our shift in the igloo.

Laughter and light poured from a dozen windows of Rathmullan House as we crept past, looking from the outside in at expensive women and affluent men ornamenting the timeless rooms. Professional laughter, gin and tonic, Vivaldi, money.

The Tasty Bite in Rathmullan played Elvis on the jukebox, so Daisy and Johnboy jived while the fish was frying. The beach-party man had told Johnboy that The Pig and Chicken had a live band so after an immature argument about the last battered onion ring we went there to hear The Boys from Ballybofey.

And better still. Bronco Bert and his Mechanical

Bull were offering £100 to the person who could stay on the bull and not get thrown off.

"Dead on," said Johnboy gulping down his pint, "If I win the £100, Daisy, I'll buy you some sexy underwear."

He was thrown off immediately. I heard Daisy say, "Flowers and chocolates only, you naughty boy."

After my effort Bronco Bert himself picked me off the airbed and said it was obvious I rode, heels down, knees up and all that but in my condition surely it was a bit dangerous?

Back at our table Johnboy was informing Daisy that her knickers were appalling and he knew they were held together with sellotape and nappy pins.

While Huge was at the bar and Daisy and Johnboy were queuing for the Bull a woman came over to advise me not to get back on, "Too dangerous in your condition, love," and suddenly it all clicked.

Everybody thought I was pregnant and my darling dungaree shorts were maternity wear. So none of us won the £100 and we stumbled home poverty-stricken.

The party was still throbbing in Rathmullan House. As we passed a woman wearing a gorgeous black sequined frock pushed through us followed closely by a half-dressed man who was shouting "Jezebel" at her.

The campfire was lit but deserted when we reached the beach. We ate Johnboy's Jaffa Cakes and Apple Puffs in its flickering light. The fire could not heat the chill air of early summer.

CHAPTER TWENTY-TWO

Considerate Huge. He wrapped me in the *pièce de résistance* sleeping-bag. We didn't know how to operate it initially and Huge was too reserved to knock on Johnboy's tent and ask him. I then realised that he had zipped me in upside-down. Over me he wound a leopard-skin rug (Aunt Maisie's) and I wore two sweaters but no socks because they had got wet in a puddle when I nipped behind a hedge for a pee.

Huge, who did not normally snore, snored. My feet became colder and colder, then my legs. The ground was hard; the tent smelled of glue.

Eventually I managed to wake Huge by sticking my tongue in his ear.

"I'm cold, Huge," apologetically, hoping he would snog me.

"Let's just hug," he said sleepily. With that there was a roar of engines, a flash of headlights and the beach party arrived. Not Hell's Angels on motorbikes, but kids in Hiace vans. I could hear them pouring out of sliding doors. Huge and I lay like mice in the inflatable igloo. I imagined the beach party setting fire to us. I imagined being gang-bang raped.

Then the kids made their first mistake. They threw

a tyre on Johnboy's tent, and Johnboy rose in wrath and seized a tent peg to use as a dagger and yelled, "What's your problem?"

Defending the Mercedes of course, not Huge or me and certainly not Daisy.

The beach party, suddenly modest, retreated to the beach and I climbed into Huge's nice quilted sleeping-bag and the boil of our two bodies together sent me to sleep immediately.

Next morning his breathing irritated me and the closeness of his body was all over me so I slid out of the sleeping-bag and out of the tent and into the gorgeous morning. The beach party had gone home. I watched the waves winking at me, heard the lapping water call me. Too much to resist. Stripped off my sweaters and my pyjamas, turned an enthusiastic cartwheel in the sand and plunged starkers into the lough.

It was the best idea I ever had. The water, cool and clean, closed round me. I swam up the path of the morning sun and felt really artistic, as if I was the first person to ever think of it.

Huge was watching from the beach.

"Come in," I yelled. "Come in."

"Come out you fool, before somebody sees you."

I almost loved him, standing sleepy on the beach, come to look for me.

Modestly he wrapped me in a blanket when I emerged.

Johnboy and Daisy had made tea which tasted of plastic. I felt happy.

"Did you notice the fortune-teller's sign beside The Pig and Chicken last night?" Daisy asked.

So she and I walked to the fortune-teller while Johnboy and Huge reclined in the sun and Johnboy explained the intricacies of his sheep-coping machine to Huge.

Madame Lolita smelled of pee and was eating strawberry yogurt. Daisy was in and out again in fifteen minutes.

"It's a fiver for your hand and ten if you want the crystal ball. The crystal will give you the initials of the man you are going to marry."

"Just a fiver's worth please," I told Madame Lolita.

"You have had great sadness," she said inspecting my lifeline. "And shed many tears for love."

Great. Other girls got tall strangers in uniform and secret admirers and a pay rise.

"You have psychic powers," continued Madame Lolita, "Trust your instincts and they will guide you. He is on your mind. You are on his mind. You must tell him that you want him."

Fat chance I thought.

"There is a third party but she means nothing to him. He will offer you a ring but you will refuse the first time."

Oh hell. Even a bit of a chat about seeing a wedding or marrying a red-haired man. Well maybe not red-haired.

"Forget the past. You can't change it," she said.

Then we did some proper fortune-telling: I was

artistic and would be successful in a creative sphere. I had a lot of admirers. Many men would love me. (At last!) When I was forty-one and a half my life would change dramatically.

I asked her if I would ever get married. That was her job after all.

She said, "Marriage has not passed you by."

I asked her if I would be happy. She didn't answer me. But as I was leaving she said, "You cannot be happy. You think too much."

I felt a goose skip over my grave.

Daisy was sitting in the sunlight eating an ice-cream. A golden child I thought poetically. While I was a woman of dark and secret passions.

"Oh Helen, she said I was very fertile and not to be taking chances. And she said that in ten months I was going to be living with a man with a ring on my finger. And my marriage was going to be the success story of my life. And I was going to rock the cradle three times."

"She said I was going to cross water," I said. "And there is money coming for me in the post."

CHAPTER TWENTY-THREE

T he arch was being stoned in Ballyronan. Aunt Louise phoned to alert daddy. Uncle Reggie had already departed to defend it with his life, should the necessity arise.

But what could daddy do? He was tired out, having cycled ten miles that afternoon on Emily. We told him to take his wellies off before he left or they would sweat his feet, but there is no telling my father anything at this time of year.

Mummy became worried. He mustn't be half well she confided in me if he wouldn't go to the arch's defence. Of course if he had gone she would have scolded for a week.

Daisy and I accompanied her to the Orange Hall on the Twelfth morning. Johnboy was an Orangeman and we were going to watch him. Uncle Reggie was collecting money and smiling at the same time. Daddy flirted with the girls who played in the band, average age twelve. Neither of them took their bowler hats off all day. Willie Simpson, chief drummer, refused to put his hat on as it would flatten his gelled crew cut. Being Johnboy's friend he tried to chat me up while Johnboy was occupied with Daisy. Willie's cavernous nostrils have always repelled me. The conversation halted abruptly when I foolishly revealed I had studied in Dublin (bastion of Popery, you recall!)

Willie was in charge of the band on the bus trip to Ballyronan. He didn't let any of them drink minerals. "You know why," he told them ominously. Instead he supplied a box of Kit-Kat and a bag of jelly babies.

"Willie, Willie," the band girls shrieked. Then Willie rattled his drum in accompaniment to Slack Alice's solo of the "Sash."

Aunt Louise and mummy had to sit together on the bus because daddy and Uncle Reggie were standing at the front directing the driver. I overheard Aunt Louise giving Uncle Reggie a tonguing because he was wearing a light-coloured suit.

Mummy, Aunt Louise, Daisy and I walked after the band like groupies. I hoped I would see no one who knew me. Daisy remained unconcerned. None of Ballyronan's high society was out, unless you can include Ian Flemming's family. Mrs Flemming remained rooted to her white plastic chair although the heavens opened above her.

Tea after the parade was an experience. A lucky dip for sandwiches cunningly concealed in white paper bags. When daddy was worshipful master he had forwarded a motion to have the sandwiches put in see-through bags so you knew what you were getting. But the lodge, ever conventional, had rebelled, and the sandwiches remained in white paper. There was no advantage to being choosy. In true picnic tradition all the sandwiches tasted of paper bag. Tinned salmon, tunafish and brown sauce, corned beef and lettuce. Wasted. The fatter the band member the more fastidious her appetite. Slack Alice, who at a conservative estimate weighed in at sixteen stones, was going through the bags in search of an egg-and-onion sandwich and no one tried to stop her.

Daisy ate four pieces of genuine carrot cake, complete with walnuts and raisins.

"It's not the first piece that makes you fat," she joked. I ate a terribly sweet caramel square and contemplated joining Henry my triangle-playing cousin. He had just vomited over the new Clarks shoes that Aunt Louise had bought him for the occasion.

Sheltering in a burger bar Daisy and I watched the platform party tune up while Johnboy gorged on burgers; he didn't eat lodge picnics. I left them alone together during the opening hymn "Oh God, Our Help in Ages Past" and phoned Laura to come and get me. Laura used to love the Twelfth. It's terrible what being a mother can do to people. I had a lot of jam to make anyway.

We commenced jam-making weeks ago. But the raspberries showed no sign of dying. And we had no jam jars left to put the jam in. I had raided the shelves in the outside loo, checked daddy's workshop in the byre and the hen-house. Then I resorted to empty coffee jars and though I poured honey, pickles, peanut butter, cranberry sauce and mayonnaise from their containers, we still didn't have enough. And mummy who had gone mad making exotic jams like rhubarb and ginger, and gooseberry said there was little point putting an ad in the paper for jars because, "there are no old-fashioned people left with jampots stored away."

So now we let the jam cool in the big saucepan and then poured it into Tupperware boxes. There is plenty of Tupperware in Derryrose because in the good old days when we had money mummy hosted Tupperware parties and we would eat up the leftover fruit flans for weeks afterwards.

Daisy returned from the Twelfth with a lovebite on her neck, and Johnboy's latest, "I want to be artistic."

"Artistic in what way?"

Aunt Maisie and Bobby Lennox had had a massive row in the field because Bobby refused to take her to the pub in Ballyronan, which was full of drunken Orangemen and warm beer. Bobby Lennox was a very fastidious drinker. Aunt Maisie had produced a tantrum, thrown her cup of tea over Bobby and marched home. She was having hysterics upstairs in her bedroom.

"Johnboy thinks we could make Yuletide logs," said Daisy who was inspecting her lovebite shamelessly. "I had no idea he was eating me."

I suggested that this was, perhaps, not the season for Yuletide logs. Daisy only laughed and said, "Silly.

We are only going to start practising now. So we will be experts by Christmas."

Daisy was of course planning to assist in every way possible. Daisy's eternal enthusiasm never failed to baffle me. Huge had been buying a new stereo system for two weeks now and already I was bored rigid hearing about it. I could not be lured into a music shop for love or money any more.

That night Huge took me home to view his new stereo. But damn him, he was playing his new compact disc by a cowboy who had died of alcohol poisoning. Over and over he played "Do You Still Have a Trace of His Love in Your Eyes?"

Played it over and over until I was ready to scream. Not even shifting could take away the picture the song made in my head. And I couldn't sleep afterwards. The noise in my head wouldn't go away.

It was the deadly silence in the kitchen that gave them away. Laura and Daisy just sitting there and not arguing. Bad sign. They both jumped as I came in and looked away again immediately. The bad news they couldn't share crushed.

"Who is it?' I said. "Who's dead?"

Aunt Maisie I thought wildly, or Granny McBride, or Jennifer. Jennifer had broken her neck riding. Her mad red horse had kicked her to death. Aunt Maisie's Mini had exploded; she had been trapped beneath the clutch and brake pedal when it had crashed and a fireman had had to shoot her so she didn't burn to death. I should stop reading tabloid newspapers.

Laura and Daisy were so silent and guilty.

Daisy handed me a postcard. Jockeys in the rain. Degas.

"You'll never believe this. I'm marrying Richard."

Elisabeth. Golden Elisabeth. Daisy and Laura and I had all lived with her in Dublin, in student days. She had known Richard through the C of I network. She was my friend. She had never wanted Richard. They had shifted once at an Ag Ball but she had always said it was a drunken mistake. He must have been mad about her, even then. Maybe he had always wanted her and had visited us in Palmerston Road to visit her. Not me. He hadn't ever wanted me. It was always Elisabeth.

"Where are mummy and daddy? Do they know?" I asked cheerfully.

"Daddy is hiding in the outside loo," said Daisy, "And mummy has locked herself in the sitting-room with *The Quiet Man*. The shithawk."

"Daisy," I was shocked. Johnboy was a bad influence on her.

"The cowardly shithawk," Daisy repeated. Shithawk was daddy's favourite swear-word, though in mixed company he said geek instead.

Daisy was very upset because Elisabeth was marrying Richard. I decided that it was wonderful for them and said so.

"I think it is wonderful for them," I said. Laura scowled. "Don't be so wet, Helen," she shouted, "It's the worst thing that could ever have happened. Them getting married."

Confused. I said, "I don't understand either of you. Why are you so upset? Richard must have been mad about her for years. You remember how often he visited Palmerston Road. I think it's marvellous."

Very firmly so they would know I meant it. I did mean it. I was delighted for her. For them.

Daisy was crying. Tears streamed down her cheeks and off the end of her chin.

"I'm disappointed in you, Daisy," I said.

"And I'm disappointed in him," Daisy screamed. "I thought he was a real man."

"He was never a real man." Laura scolded instead of crying. "He never came to Helen when she was dying. He never rocked the boat. He hadn't the nerve. I knew he would do something like this in the end."

I stood up.

"I'm going to write to Elisabeth and congratulate her," I said, "Maybe she will invite us then." And I walked out of the kitchen with my head held high.

"You'll never believe this. I'm marrying Richard."

Elisabeth's letter was easy to write. And I rooted in the big attic for a photograph I had of her and Richard. We had gone racing to Punchestown with a boyfriend of hers. And Elisabeth, who knew nothing of betting or form, had won a fortune on the first race. She had been queuing at the tote determined to back Cock Cockburn so she could shout "Come on, Cock" from the stands. A leprechaun in front of her told her to back No. 3; he had had a tip from the stables.

So in true Elisabethan style she had put all her pocket-money on the tipped horse who was a sad outsider and instantly forgettable in the parade ring. And the appalling animal had romped home. I photographed Richard rescuing her hat that she had lobbed in the air when the tipped horse won.

Alas poor Richard, I knew him well!

I hoped Daisy and Laura weren't going to pity me because Elisabeth was marrying Richard.

CHAPTER TWENTY-FOUR

E lisabeth phoned. She was in Dublin working, she said. I was sceptical. Never in living memory had Elisabeth indulged in industrious endeavour. Elisabeth was an ornamental tart.

She wanted me to come to Dublin as she fancied a girls' night out. "Here you are," she said. "Richard wants to talk to you," followed by sounds of protest from Richard.

"Hello Helen, how are you?" bland, distant, well-camouflaged.

I was rash and flippant in my congratulations. But we didn't talk, just comments thrown at random, without intimacy. I was relieved when he handed me back to Elisabeth.

"Of course, he won't be here next week." I heard her giggle. Standoffish Richard was probably undressing her as she talked to me. Elisabeth had a testosterone-inducing effect on asexual men. "He is depressed with the vulgarity of the Horse Show last week."

"I'll be there."

Vulgarity indeed. Hanging up, I cycled Emily along the Toomestone Road to the shop run by Catholics

and bought salt-and-vinegar flavoured peanuts and
fizzy mineral. Mummy was in the chip shop next
door, a towel wrapped turban style round her head.
Protecting her bleached hair from the sun. Vulgar
too I suppose. I went in to join her.

"Go away," she shouted from the front of the shop
in front of the other customers and the shop girl,
"You aren't getting any of my chips. I'm going to
hide in Beauty and eat them all myself."

She had a cleg bite on her neck that looked like
Daisy's lovebite.

"I want to go to Dublin on the train on Wednesday
morning," I explained, "Elisabeth phoned."

"Oh, her." Mummy sniffed.

"Will you take me to the train if I buy you the fish
and chips?"

Mummy was late coming back from leaving Laura to
the dole office on Wednesday morning. I was slightly
nervous and played ELO's "Out of Control" at full
blast through the house. I had put on all my make-
up to cover a scrab on my nose that Huge had caused
when we were last in bed together.

Mummy had to rally Beauty on to catch the train.
I raced to the desk where a well-dressed Englishman
was footering with his cheque book.

"Jesus Christ," I muttered, desperate to go to the
loo and wanting to buy Elisabeth a bottle of wine
before boarding. "The incompetence of men." Maybe
he didn't hear me. I sounded like Sarah. It reminded

me of the first time I met Huge's mother. She had described me as "tall, good-looking and intimidating." I was not any of those things.

On the train I checked my hair was still pinned up, powdered my nose four times and after a cup of railway coffee relipsticked my mouth. Why did I feel so nervous?

Summer in Dublin. I took the 46A to Mount Merrion where Elisabeth was living and wandered aimlessly up and down North and South Avenue searching for Cedar Mount Road. My face powder melted, my marvellously pinned up hair collapsed and no one knew where Cedar Mount Road was.

I was swilling Guinness in Mount Merrion House and feeling sorry for myself when Elisabeth herself floated in. She was delighted to see me and I was flattered. She never changes, Elisabeth.

Of course I asked her about Richard. She looked like thick whipped cream. She asked me about Huge. I smiled knowingly.

We had a magnificent girls' night out with Chinese food and wine and girly chat.

"I remember writing in my diary," I said, "when I was sixteen and going out with Mark Taylor, 'I have started to enjoy French kissing. Now I fight back with my tongue.'"

And I told her of the Christmas Daisy went out with a plumber called Derek who rolled on top of her in the car and said, "Make a bad boy out of me."

And she told me of a hot boyfriend who had been

mauling her and she had grabbed him by the willie and said, "One more move and I'm pulling it off."

We reached the somewhat cynical conclusion that girls only get engaged so they can screw with a clear conscience.

I'm sure she gave me coffee with caffeine in it before bed. We shared her big bouncy double bed and because I was cold she made me put my legs in the arms of her Puffa. But I still couldn't sleep so I slipped into the sitting-room, ate a 90g bag of cheese-and-onion crisps in twenty-five seconds and fell unconscious on the sloping sofa.

Maybe Elisabeth did have gainful employment. When I rose she had departed leaving a written decree that we would "do lunch."

I decided on cheese on toast for breakfast. Wrong decision. I sawed through my finger trying to slice the cheese. And on the wireless I heard there had been a massive bomb in Magherafelt. Hell. I would have to phone home and express concern.

Mummy said she had heard nothing—she had been too busy shouting—but Laura had piled the twins into Beauty about nine and driven off. Gone in search of a bit of excitement. When the bomb drops, Laura, instead of hightailing it into the bunker with the rest of us and the tinned beef stew (19p, Wellworths Sale), will stand out and watch it all exploding around her.

Elisabeth's flatmate, Angela (a real goer), had returned from her daily five-mile run as I settled with the *Irish Times* crossword and a pot of lemon tea. She insisted that I take the sticky plaster off the mutilated finger, to let it breathe. An SAS type she wrapped the finger in a hanky and sellotaped the whole thing together.

"You are making a problem out of a situation," she told me severely when I tried to protest. She was tall, good-looking and intimidating. I didn't have a chance.

"So," she asked me after fifty press-ups and an ice-cold shower, "what are you doing with yourself, Helen?" Angela was doing a PhD in nuclear physics.

"I have been bee-keeping in the Yemen," I said. "Great place, piles of culture, but too hot for me. It's my fair skin. It burns easily. I'm going to Venezuela to work as a rancher in the autumn."

Angela was fascinated. "I suppose it gives you inspiration for your novels?"

"Yes. Actually I must get ready. I'm meeting my publishers for lunch. In the Shelbourne. They are sending a taxi for me."

I pulled on my coat and walked to Rathmines second-hand bookshop where the owner gave me a guided tour of the science-fiction department and told me he would be happy to help advise should I desire (him or the books?). I stuck to what I knew and bought *One Hundred Years of Solitude*.

Elisabeth and I "did lunch" in Bewleys. "I think I've been robbed," I told her. "£2 for a bottle of water and a sticky bun."

"Sadly, no," said Elisabeth, "Tradition is so bloody expensive these days."

Elisabeth had no engagement ring on her finger but I didn't like to ask. Probably Richard's ring was a priceless heirloom and was locked away in a bank vault.

"Oh yes," she laughed, her eyes following my eyes to her empty finger. "I've been saving this story. The night Richard popped the question he gave me a ring. I wrapped it in a paper hanky and put it in my pocket."

"As you would," I said sarcastically.

"Indeed. Do you know what I did? I threw the paper hanky down the loo when I got home and flushed the ring away. Accidentally of course. So I don't have an engagement ring now and Richard naturally refuses to buy me another."

Huge joined me in Dublin on Friday. He looked stressed. No sane woman would be bothered with a successful man, Merc or no Merc. Huge gave his job so much sometimes there was nothing left for me. He was very taken with Elisabeth.

"But everyone loves Elisabeth," he protested in bed. Angela the real goer had gone hill-walking in the Burren so we had taken her bedroom. It was a tight squeeze in the narrow maidish bed. Huge turned his back to me, taking most of the blankets with him. "That's what you have been telling me since she got engaged, 'But everybody loves Elisabeth, Huge.' Repeat to fade."

I decided I was not glad to see him after all.

"I wish," I said crossly tugging at the sheet, "that blankets were like loo roll. You could pull them up as far as you wanted and then rip off the bits that you don't need."

Huge's humour had not returned the next morning. He had been beastly like this for a couple of weeks now, since Elisabeth had written to me of her engagement. As if he was just going through the motions of dating me. And he took the last three inches of bathwater and didn't ask me to join him as he usually did.

Elisabeth said, "Richard is coming up this evening for a party. Why don't we have dinner together beforehand? We could go to the Bad Ass café and drink lots of red wine."

Richard had never gone to parties when he was my friend. He had despised them.

Afterwards Huge said, "So you don't like this Richard Knight that she's marrying? You were very off when she suggested we go out together."

And later: "Pull yourself together, Helen, please, and stop sulking. Elisabeth is very decent to have us to stay. The least we can do is buy her dinner."

"Please stop telling me how wonderful Elisabeth is," I asked finally.

Dinner at the Bad Ass with Richard. And Elisabeth and Huge. I drank three glasses of red wine in a row and it wasn't so awful. Spoke when spoken to and drank wine when he spoke to anybody else. Richard didn't look euphoric or fulfilled. He still looked dour, Richard-like. He asked for my mother and Aunt Maisie. He had seen Charlie and George Montgomery at the Horse Show. No Jennifer. She had pulled the short straw and was at Kinelvin with the baby.

"Richard knows my sister's husband," I told Huge.

"I think you have drunk enough," he said back again.

After dinner Richard and Elisabeth went to the party and Huge and I took a taxi back to Mount Merrion. Huge sat in the front and discussed imported automatic Japanese cars with the taxi driver. He ignored me.

I was asleep when we got to Cedar Mount Road and he had to carry me into the house. Vaguely, far away I heard the taximan say, "She might have had a bit much to drink."

Huge dumped me on Angela's bed. I dreamed torture. Richard and I were running away. He was sitting outside in the car waiting for me. It was lashing rain but I had to find Henry before I left. The rain pounded on the windows and Richard was waiting and I couldn't find Henry. And Richard drove off without me.

I woke fully dressed, boots and all. My mouth tasted like the inside of a sewer and my head was bursting though I had no headache. And Huge wasn't friends with me. He must have had a hangover. Drinking always makes Huge crabbed.

We went for breakfast in Bewleys.

"Take that stupid bandage off your finger," he commanded, "and stand and wait for the tea while I get myself toast."

I didn't like his attitude.

"Now go and get that table by the fire while I pay."

"Did you get me anything?" I asked when he sat down and began eating.

"Tea." He nodded towards it.

"Did you get me lemon?"

He ignored me. He knew that I couldn't drink tea without lemon. Elegantly I stood up, lifted his plate of Irish Fry and tipped it over his handsome head.

"You bastard," I said turning on my heel, ignoring the gaping mouths of the nice people at the neighbouring table. Huge caught up with me at the Boer War memorial on Stephen's Green. No kindness from Huge today. He dragged me to the car and drove in silent fury back to Mount Merrion. I had forgotten what a non-exhibitionist person Huge tried to be.

"You immature, temperamental, sulky brat," he shouted as he dragged me into the flat. "You have behaved disgracefully all weekend. You sulk with Elisabeth, you get drunk last night, you make a fool of yourself in Bewleys. What's the matter with you?"

I spat in his face and he slapped me hard so I fell back onto the sofa. Nobody, not even mummy, had ever slapped me across the face. Huge stood over me.

"Pack your bags. You're coming home with me."

"I don't want to go anywhere with you." I was

blind with tears. I knew what was happening. Things were never going to be the same again.

"Very well. I have no pity for you, Helen. God knows I have tried to get through to you. I don't want to try any more."

"You have been cold for days," I cried, furious with my tears. The mutilated finger, that he had made me take the bandage off, was bleeding again.

"And you closed me out," he said.

In the end I did pack my bags and leave with him. It would have been stupid and proud to take the hated bus. We didn't speak once in the car. He played his album with the song "Do You Still Have a Trace of His Love in Your Eyes?" I thought he must really like it to buy the cassette as well as I cried in the corner of the passenger seat.

CHAPTER TWENTY-FIVE

T he brown-and-white bungalow was built. But not paid for. The day Tom Johnston came looking for his money mummy hid in the byre and set Trevvie the Killer Rooster on him, and daddy was observed escaping from a downstairs window and winging his way across the potato field. Crouching behind the orchard wall I watched Tom make friends with Henry—the only one of us brave enough to tackle him. "Take me to your leader," said Tom. Tom was a man to be reckoned with.

Positive action was called for. Sadly Derryrose had already disposed of all her liquid assets in the past to make ends meet. Anything that moved had been shot for food; anything that stood still long enough was axed for firewood. And still we starved from hunger and cold. Short of selling ourselves there was no way of making money. And that left the obvious solution. Either someone got a job or we sold the farm.

So mummy performed the impossible and got herself a job. My mother has a marvellous gift. She is the first to admit that she was behind the door when academic brilliance was being handed out but she has the most incredible faculty for gaining employment when she wants it. Having taken the one "sail" on Gypsy she entered "riding" as her hobby on the application form and was called for interview. With the ingenuity of Scarlett O'Hara dressing in her mother's curtains she wore a sophisticated dress (borrowed from Sarah), Laura blew-dry her hair, I did her make-up, Daisy polished her shoes and she got the first job she applied for.

"I think the other girls in the office are Catholic," she told us when she came home, triumphant, from the interview. "They are called Bernie, Patricia, and Siobhan. So we should have a bit of crack. Of course, I would prefer a job with no responsibility, like folding knickers in Wellworths, but I have my reputation to consider.

"I really think," she added, "that you should get yourself a job too, Helen. You are becoming introverted."

This because I had spent a lonely week nursing my bruised face and telling people I had walked into a wall (drunk) in Dublin.

Derryrose had to be cleaned before she started work and Beauty had to be fixed. For Beauty was as much bother as the retired Morris. Johnboy diagnosed distributor-cap trouble and promised Daisy a court on Saturday night after he replaced it. Dateless, I had a gallery seat for the ensuing pantomime.

Mummy expressed polite interest but was mad to get back to the sitting-room where she was fitting on clothes for Monday. Daisy expressed deplorable interest as always and stood at his elbow with an old towel in case he wanted to wipe his hands.

"Pliers," commanded Surgeon Jackson and Nurse Gordon scuttled into daddy's workshop to hunt them out. There was a scream and she scuttled out again.

"Would a paintbrush do instead Johnboy? Trevvie the Killer Rooster just tried to eat me."

Finally daddy left the sitting-room, where he was constructively criticising mummy's dress sense, and went out to assist. All enthusiasm gone since her brush with Trevvie Daisy joined me in my bedroom where I was reading Virginia Woolf and discovering I had highbrow tendencies. Without ceremony or introduction she stripped off her skirt and jumper to reveal a white lace body-stocking contraption.

"Johnboy tired of the idea of Yuletide logs," she explained. "He has decided on embroidery instead. He did the pink roses and I fixed the lace.

"Poor Johnboy," she sighed. "He really wanted to impress mummy by replacing the distributor cap. He's ashamed to admit he doesn't know the firing order of a Ford.

"And he can't phone anyone either," she added.

The infamous Derryrose payphone had met a smashing end. Just before the Twelfth daddy demanded that mummy open the phone and give him the money inside to pay his lodge subscription fees. When mummy refused he had thrown a wobbly, ripped the cord from the wall and smashed the phone on the kitchen floor. We were back with the phone lock again and mummy got a loan of Sarah's chastity belt to carry the key.

The morning mummy started work was stressful for everybody. Conservatively dressed in lilac she handbrake-turned at the bottom of the drive and raced back into the house.

"I have forgotten something, Helen," she announced. "What is it?"

Appointed ladies maid I guessed hopefully, "Earrings? Watch? Lipstick?"

"Useless." She dashed back out again, wobbling slightly on her new white peep-toe slingbacks.

I was clearing the breakfast dishes when I realised that it was her lunchbox. For years she had sent us to school with cheese sandwiches. Her lunchbox was filled with quiche and cocktail sausages and chocolate biscuits. I bet she had the chocolate biscuits hidden in her handbag with everything else. The pliers had been produced from her handbag on Saturday night along with a hammer, two screwdrivers and a curling brush. Everything except a purseful of money.

I ate a biscuit and thought about getting a job. A few months bee-keeping in the Yemen might cure me of Richard and Huge. I might meet a rich Arab who would seduce me into his harem where I would become fat and brown and wear silk on my shoulders and a ruby in my navel. I could bath in asses' milk and not have to make do with recycled bathwater as at present. A harem suggested sanctuary.

My sisters and I were invited to Sandra Flemming's (*née* Jackson) new home that evening. Sandra, home from a month honeymooning in Disney World, had been inviting us to visit her for weeks. Ian, already an accountant and lay-preacher, had become a partner in the fitted-bathroom empire on his marriage and he and Sandra had bought a house in Ballyronan beside Castle Flemming, his parents' country-seat.

"I told Ian this carpet was too expensive," Sandra told us. "£30 a square yard, you know. And the underfelt was £5 a square yard. 'Ian,' I said, 'this carpet is too expensive.' But he insisted. He says you can always tell synthetic fibres."

"Yes," we all agreed. Mummy had bought a new carpet for the sitting-room when Laura got married but it had only cost £3 a square yard, on the stalls at the May Fair in Magherafelt.

"It matches your wallpaper," I offered. I found houses a lot easier to admire than children. Sandra's wallpaper was very flash, dark red with blue and gold gilt flowers traced on it.

"Yes," said Sandra. "The paper is dark of course but this is such a large room and has so many windows..."

"It's a pity," said Sarah who had remained silent up to this, "that the seams are so obvious in dark wallpaper.

"And why," she added, "do you have no lampshade in here?"

Sandra puffed importantly. "I haven't seen

anything just right yet. I was in Brown Thomas on Saturday but they had nothing. I'll know my lampshade when I see it."

"Did your mother make the curtains, Sandra?" Sarah asked.

"Mummy? Of course not. We bought the fabric in Harrods when we stopped in London on the way home from Disney. They made them up while Ian and I were in the waxworks."

To give Sandra her due the bronze statue of the naked men was predominantly displayed on one of the half-dozen occasional tables scattered artistically about the room. I was sure she would hide it again once we left.

We filtered through the spotless house; you wouldn't have found dust with a sniffer dog.

"White is always right," she explained of the blinding bathroom. "So says my interior decorator."

"And I suppose this person also says that plants give a room character?" Sarah asked through the cheeseplant jungle on the edge of the fitted bath. "Is this bath marble?"

"Do Ian and you bath together?" Laura asked her and the Rabbit blushed.

"Ian waters the plants with cold tea," she said stroking her Mother-in-Law's Tongue and racing us on to the kitchen with its Olde Worlde glass-windowed cupboards and its jawbox sink unit. We used to have a jawbox sink in Derryrose but, ever unfashionable, we now had stainless steel.

"Oh the beams are marvellous," Daisy and I said together.

"Are they polystyrene from Texas?" Sarah again.

"Sandblasted," said Sandra, very serious, "And stained."

"And now," said Sandra, "This is a very special occasion. We got our wedding video back this morning and I want you to be the first to see it."

To relive, to sit through the most meaningful day of Sandra's life. And not even a drink to help.

The powder-blue frills of the chauffeur's shirt; Ian's mother's cleaning lady's next-door neighbour's daughter; flower girl tripping on the train at the front of the church and banging her nose on the communion table; the dreadful droning prayer of Rev Robinson who was better at funerals than weddings; the singer Mrs Flemming had flown in from Wales and tried to pass off as a distant cousin.

It was riotous but Sandra never saw satire and couldn't understand what we were laughing about.

"Jackie's speech was beautiful," she anticipated her father-in-law's contribution. "Perfect sentence structure."

"Thank you, Ian, for being our son."

Surely it was time she fed us?

Mrs Flemming Junior produced a tiny silver tray of salmon on brown bread. And a plate of deep-fried walnuts and curried almonds. And a dish of marinated artichoke hearts and asparagus canapés.

I would have killed for a ham sandwich and a

glass of Guinness.

Finally she produced a bottle of non-alcoholic wine and perfect brandy snaps.

"Do you think I have changed since I got married?" she asked as we were leaving.

"No," we reassured her.

"Mummy says I laugh all the time now," she said.

CHAPTER TWENTY-SIX

Mummy was relaxing at home after a hard day at the office and daddy was carrying her cups of tea and massaging her shoulders. Licking envelopes and posting letters can be an endless occupation.

"Of course it was only initiation today," said mummy pompously. "Tomorrow I get a desk and filing-cabinet of my own. And a time-share on a word processor."

Actually mummy was riding the sympathy train because she carried a guilty secret. The notorious Ruth and her toyboy Sid had bought and renovated their council house in Magherafelt. And were having a party on Saturday to celebrate.

And Ruth had invited mummy a week ago and mummy had accepted on behalf of herself and daddy, and daddy didn't know yet and when he found out he would throw a wobbly and refuse to go because he hated Ruth and was afraid of Ruth's Bohemian friends.

Mummy employed many sinister and macabre tactics designed at husband husbandry. But daddy, easily manipulated in most fields of domestic battle, always drew the line at Ruth Paisley.

So mummy bounced strategies off us when she

required a cunning plan. She thought it would make us cute so we could work our own husbands if and when they finally materialised.

"If he goes," she said, "he will sleep in a corner all night."

"At least he won't be boisterous," we said thinking of Uncle Reggie who always insisted on singing when he visited, and who became distinctly lecherous after a can of beer.

"But," mummy continued, "he won't kiss anyone else's wife. He says all Ruth's friends are AIDS carriers."

Since the outbreak of AIDS awareness daddy kept his toothbrush in his sock drawer and always took his own glass when he went to the pub.

"He could talk to Cecil Simpson," Daisy suggested. "They could get drunk and waltz together like they used to."

"Cecil Simpson has one redeeming feature," said mummy. "If you throw him a packet of crisps it keeps him occupied for half an hour. Slack Alice always keeps a supply with her. Ruth is such a brilliant cook. She had steak at the last party, just before the Twelfth last year when your father felt confident enough to attend. He even ate the steak without complaining, and you know he says it always sticks between his teeth. It was Ruth's birthday and Sid dressed up as a Strip-O-Gram and Ruth ate the string…"

She stopped. There are things even the most liberated mother can't reveal.

"Anyway it disgusted your father. He's becoming

a bore."

"It's since he was voted on to the church committee," said Daisy. "He wouldn't let me wear my new bra-top to the Port with Johnboy last week."

Daddy refused to go to Ruth's party. He had made other arrangements. The church committee had organised a treasure hunt and barbeque in Drum Manor forest park and daddy had bought the tickets already.

"Go and phone Ruth immediately, Jennifer," he instructed. "And tell her we aren't going."

"But I want to go," mummy protested. She had had a hard day at the office. "Go you and phone Adam and tell him we can't go to the barbeque. He might give you your money back, though I doubt it."

"No," said daddy and so began the greatest row my parents ever had. Differences of opinion and friendly battles of will forgotten. This was warfare. I pitched my allegiance firmly on the fence and made a run for it on the approach of either of them.

Mummy said she was going to Ruth's party alone.

"Unchaperoned?" I asked aghast. It was Saturday night. Daddy, dressed in cream-and-white socks and a yellow shirt, had just driven off to the barbeque with Sarah.

"Yes," said mummy parading in front of me in the trousers you can see her knicker-line through and her three-inch black stilettos. I had been swigging gooseberry wine all day and as mummy and daddy were completely engrossed in each other no one noticed I was becoming an alcoholic.

"What about flatter heels?" I suggested gently.

"No, your father has to learn."

Mummy in her rebellious rush to Ruth's had left the telephone unlocked. A most insane idea shot through my head. I would lock myself in the sitting-room and phone Richard.

Fool.

How I wanted someone to talk to. But I couldn't phone Richard because he didn't want me. And I couldn't phone Huge because he had left me.

I phoned Huge but he wasn't in. I hadn't really expected him to be. I didn't leave a message on his answering machine.

Mummy slept in Aunt Maisie's bed when she got home from the party. Daddy had waited up for her. I heard them shouting at each other.

"I hate you," yelled mummy.

"I hate you too," yelled daddy.

Next morning neither went to church. When we got home there was no dinner made and mummy was refusing to get out of bed. Daddy was in the sitting-room watching *She Wore A Yellow Ribbon*, Laura had bought him the video for Christmas. It had got to the bit where Big John was retiring from the cavalry and was being presented with a gold watch. Daddy was weeping copiously.

"This couldn't be good for us," commented Daisy. "No wonder we are so odd, with the example they show. They never stop fighting."

"I heard them yelling at each other last night," I

said. "And they are sleeping in separate beds."

"I think," said Daisy, "that it is time for us to run away again."

On Wednesday night Johnboy took Daisy and me to the Arts Theatre. It had been raining all day and Johnboy phoned after the milking to say he wasn't going to "dress up" because of the weather. He was going to wear his Val Doonican style Aran jumper instead.

"Johnboy," I heard Daisy's little voice. "Johnboy I might be wrong but I don't think it rains in theatres." Daisy had never really accepted mummy's theories on man management but she always got her own way with her own methods.

Johnboy looked dashing in a shirt and tie, and Daisy looked very elegant in her flowery Jigsaw dress, shortened to reveal her great legs.

"I'm going to marry a girl with legs like yours," Charlie Montgomery had told her once when they were going out together. And he had. He had married Jennifer, the sister.

I wore my Laura Ashley dress which was green and suitable because I felt like a gooseberry.

At the interval I saw Huge. With a very beautiful girl, who was obviously not wearing an Age Concern dress.

Daisy and Johnboy were arguing as to who should go for the ice-cream.

"Stand there, Johnboy, and talk to Helen. I'll get it."

"No, Daisy. You will be crushed in the queue. I'll go."

"What a stupid argument," I said. "I'll go." I didn't want Huge to see me.

Daisy was chatting to Huge when I returned, entertaining him with a grossly exaggerated account of my swoon at the abattoir that morning.

A farmer's daughter, and an agricultural scientist, I was not of the squeamish persuasion.

"She can't feel a thing," Daisy comforted as bewildered Betty, a cow we had had for years, was chased into the box and stunned. I nodded toughly when a hugely fat man who must have been an amoeba in another life sliced at her throat. But a flicker of the light of vegetarianism flashed at me when her blood bounced out.

It was at the skinning machine that I disgraced myself. I had watched a woman with tattooed arms chainsaw her in half. I had watched her ears being chopped off. But I swooned before I got the chance to see her skin being torn from her, so I missed that bit. A black cloud closed and when the cloud cleared I was in the head vet's office with a bump on the back of the head. Daisy said it was just as well I had tipped over backwards or I would have been washed down the chute with Betty's entrails.

Huge smiled politely and introduced Victoria Waugh. How long after me had he taken her?

"Huge, darling," I said, "Could you post me my copy of *Lady Chatterley's Lover*? I think I left it in your bed."

I thought the second half of the play dragged terribly. My feet were cold and I kept nodding off to sleep. At the end I clapped loudly because it was the end.

I had been dreaming of Huge. He had cooked me dinner and made a joke about how lucky I was to have a warm house to come to and dinner cooked for me.

And I said, "Don't give me that marriage chat."

And he said, "You must be joking, Helen. I am never going to marry you. How many times do I have to tell you?"

And I had demanded to know what was wrong with me that he wouldn't marry me. "We fight well," I said. "We love well. We go out to places well. Why won't you marry me?"

I might have called him Richard. I'm not sure.

On the way home I drifted in and out of sleep, and Daisy and Johnboy decided to become actors. Johnboy reckoned he had the exhibitionism and confidence required. By the time we reached Toomestone they had remembered a notice in the local paper the previous week encouraging people to join Magherafelt's amateur drama society.

"Maybe the notice will be in again this week," said Daisy. "I'll check the paper tomorrow. Helen, will you come too?"

"He left me," I said, "for an anorexic blonde who drips in gold jewellery and looks perfectly useless in bed. And why? Because I'm smarter than him. And I wear Oxfam clothes. And I don't like his friends. I'm quite upset."

"Why?" asked Daisy.

"Because we were so good together in bed. I hate it when sex and money aren't enough. I had become rather fond of him too. He was so solid when he hugged me. This is so unpleasant. I hate having to face unpleasant things. I'd rather sweep them under the carpet. I know I used his razor to shave my legs. I know I never made the bed when we got out of it. He expected me to make the bed. But I built his bloody garden for him. He didn't know the difference between lilac and lavender until he met me. I mean," I finished as we got out at Derryrose. "I mean I was in love with him when I remembered."

CHAPTER TWENTY-SEVEN

T hursday stretched and stretched ahead of me, from my bed at 7.30 a.m. How was I going to fill it?

At the far side of the bedroom the plaid carpet-bag I had taken to Dublin lay, Miss Havisham style, still zipped and waiting to be emptied. I suppose I should have stopped the clock as well.

Drank my tea with *A Passionate Man*. How I wished I had my hands on a passionate man!

I was not frustrated. I was lonely.

Not a soft touch. A soft rot.

No wonder Laura lay in bed all day. No wonder Sarah went cheerfully to work. No wonder I was so bored.

But today was the day the bomb dropped on Derryrose. It was mummy's birthday and the anniversary of Kenneth's death. Kenneth was our brother and the skeleton in the Gordon cupboard.

Kenneth was born three miscarriages after Jennifer and we had been present at his birth.

Mummy wore a face of relief because Kenneth meant she wouldn't have to get pregnant again. Daddy bought her flowers because his Orange friends had teased him for years that he wasn't man enough to produce a son. Mummy had been very sick with Kenneth and every time she was taken into hospital Laura convinced us she was going to die, and morbidly wanted to be the new mummy. She imagined she would do a better job than either Gran Gran or Granny McBride who were madly jealous of each other and bought popularity with falsefaces, Easter eggs and even valentine cards.

The day Kenneth was born mummy had indigestion. Daisy and Tiger-Lily our cat had strayed on to the main road but it was Tiger-Lily, not Daisy, who got run over by a UDR Landrover. Laura was smacked for calling Daisy a "little bastard"—Laura was in with a bad crowd at primary school. While we scraped Tiger-Lily off the road and into a plastic bag for burial Jennifer escaped into the bathroom and shaved her arms with daddy's razor.

About midnight, after mummy had searched the house for the tea-towel Sarah took to bed with her and couldn't sleep without, she had time to realise that the indigestion was actually labour pains. She sent daddy to phone the midwife and Dr Hunt, because the security gates were on in Magherafelt and she didn't want a repeat performance of Jennifer's birth, on the side of the street, with half the police force in attendance. Mummy, having lost faith in the cry, "Pregnant woman coming through," had resigned herself to home birth.

Derryrose had no telephone in the '70s so daddy

walked four fields to our neighbours McMullens, and then another three fields to the public phone box on the Toomestone road because all the McMullens had gone to bed and left their Alsatian running loose.

When he eventually returned Laura had woken Daisy and me and we were in bed with mummy, keeping her entertained. Mrs Slattery the midwife was drunk and Dr Hunt had gone to deliver somebody else's baby.

"Oh well," said mummy, "Make me a cup of tea instead, Kenneth."

"Does daddy cut you open?" I asked. Sarah and Jennifer were still asleep. They were too young to appreciate the facts of life.

"Lorraine Millar told me her mother farted and the baby shot out," announced Laura.

"We must do something about your language," said mummy mildly. "Stop crying Daisy. Daddy doesn't have to cut me open."

Kenneth was wet and red when he was born. It wasn't disgusting, just interesting, like Tiger-Lily after the Landrover had squashed her and her guts were all over the road. Even Daisy stopped crying. And daddy gave us all a drink of poteen to celebrate.

Gran Gran was furious that we had been allowed to watch and that daddy hadn't called her, so she could come and be bossy.

"Contamination of their minds," she had scolded, "And Margaret is odd enough as it is."—because Daisy had an imaginary friend she always talked to.

At Kenneth's christening Granny McBride slipped in her new shoes and dropped Kenneth on his head. He died later of a bloodclot in his brain. Granny McBride tried to drown herself in the bath. She has been in the old people's home ever since.

Henry and I got out of bed about 9 o'clock to go shopping with mummy for her birthday present.

"Honest to God, Helen," she said in the jewellery shop, "I think you are anorexic," because my fingers were so thin all the silver rings were too large. Mummy would prefer me to be ten stones and take more exercise. She feels safer with strapping daughters like Laura and Daisy. To please her I bought a Pre-Raphaelite print of a Greek nymphette sitting beside a pile of food. I had suggested the *La Belle Dame Sans Merci* print but when I loosely translated it for her as The Beautiful Bitch she didn't want it. She and daddy were still at war.

I offered to bake a birthday cake but mummy said no. She wanted garlic mushrooms with ham and cheese instead. Ruth had made them for her barbeque party. But I could make the dinner instead. We decided that she would make the garlic mushrooms and I would make lasagne, coleslaw, garlic bread and lemon mousse because daddy would eat none of this food. At least cooking would fill in the hours for me. I would rather wash dishes today than brood.

But it didn't work out that way. Mummy was frying her mushrooms and I was chopping onions when daddy stormed into the kitchen roaring and waving the local paper round his head; he was having a wobbly.

Mummy had left his name off Kenneth's *In Memoriam* notice in the paper. "Fondly remembered by mummy, Laura, Helen, Daisy, Sarah and Jennifer."

It was the straw that broke the camel's back. I went upstairs because I had a huge horrible lump in my throat that couldn't be swallowed.

I was emptying Miss Havisham's carpet-bag when Daisy joined me. Ripping my clothes from the past and stuffing them into cupboards of the present.

"I can't bear it here any more," I said but she didn't hear me.

We took Henry and Gypsy and the gun to the flat meadow. Riding practice and target practice. Gypsy still wouldn't canter. I still couldn't shoot straight.

"Henry," I said when Daisy and Gypsy trotted off down the field, "Henry I can't bear it here any more."

McMullens have always kept Alsatians. And they have always taken the liberty to exercise them in our meadows, invariably after our sheep. Poor Henry who was an uncharacteristically friendly terrier must have bounded up on one in innocence and, when I noticed, it was too late. The Alsatian had Henry by the throat and was shaking him when I turned round. The way Henry shook the rats he caught. Rats screamed too, the way Henry was screaming.

I loaded the gun and shot the big dog. Dead.

A man came running across the flat meadow, a McMullen I suppose, waving his arms, roaring. Like daddy in the kitchen when he discovered mummy had left his name off the *In Memoriam* notice for Kenneth. Roaring like Huge when he hit me in Elisabeth's Dublin flat. I loaded the shotgun and steadied it against my shoulder.

"I'm marrying Richard...And you closed me out...I can't bear it here any more," I said.

Stop, Helen. Stop! Mummy and daddy in paper hats, dancing a jig in the kitchen on Christmas Day.

Stop, Helen. Stop! Huge on the sand of Lough Swilly that sun-filled camping morning.

Stop Helen. Stop! Elisabeth in her golden tapestry dress, her waterfall hair.

Daisy was galloping Gypsy from the far side of the flat meadow, galloping fat Gypsy who wouldn't gallop.

Shouting "Stop Helen. Stop!"

To save the man and to save me.

"I can't bear you any more, Richard," I said loudly, and suddenly Daisy swept by me on the runaway Gypsy and I lowered the gun, head hot with tears, bewildered by myself and my mood. Richard was right about psychotic women in the Gordon family.

Daisy finally got Gypsy pulled up at the top of the beech lane and when she got back to me the McMullen man had bolted, in case I reconsidered, I suppose, and shot him anyway. Henry's blood was warm and sticky and Daisy took him very gently and

very firmly from my arms and told me very gently
and very firmly that he was dead. She wrapped him
in her anorak and I cried as if my heart would break.
Roared and cried like a banshee. It was very
embarrassing to think of it afterwards.

I cried because more than Henry was dead.

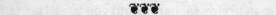